I0580293

A COMPILATION OF FANTASTICAL
FUN AND DARK TALES

WHACKY, WHIMSICAL & DARK

SEAN M. T. SHANAHAN

Copyright © 2024 by Sean M. T. Shanahan – First Edition
Copyright © 2025 by Sean M. T. Shanahan – Second Edition

All rights reserved. No part of this book may be reproduced or used in any manner without written permission of the copyright owner except for the use of quotations in a book review. For more information, address: sean@seanmts.com

Second Edition

www.seanmts.com

Cover design and formatting by Miblart.
Print ISBN: 978-1-923413-03-0

DUEL OF THE GUN WIZARDS

"You are beaten."

"What?" Gyle was overextended, his gun stance toppling forward without the push of his fire-bullet spell to keep him standing in place. He fell onto the damp, dusty earth.

His enemy, Hrothgar, chuckled as he pranced forward. "Oh, that is a pity. Did you think your gun magic would work?" he flourished and spun.

His robes twirled in a miasma of conjuring magic and he fired a bolt of lightning from the barrel of his pistol.

The bolt shot out from his weapon and tore through the damp air with an ear rendering roar before the magically infused bullet struck the ruined cathedral ceiling and crumbled stone.

Gyle pushed himself up and struck a gathering pose. He spread his stance in the dirt and summoned the arcane magic to channel into the bullet chambered in his revolver . . . but nothing happened. The arcane forces refused to respond to his call.

"You might be wondering what's happened?" Hrothgar struck several complex poses, dancing through the arcane summon poses to channel magic into a fletchette blast from his pistol. One piece of shrapnel was infused in acid, another in fire, and another in ice. All bullets struck the ground around Gyle as he tried in frustration to conjure his own gun magic. "You see, I laced your water with an inhibiting agent, nullifying your gun magic for the next day or so . . . plenty of time to slaughter you in this duel."

Gyle struck another series of poses, struggling through the drugs to conjure *something*. But nothing answered his desperate call. "Then finish it!"

"Oh, I will!" Hrothgar spun and shot out a beam of light, incinerating the pillar on the other side of Gyle.

The fiend is toying with me . . . And with that thought, Gyle felt a glimmer of hope. A solution formulated in his mind.

"Are you serious?" Gyle asked, quietly.

"Oh?" Hrothgar halted during his second pose, the magic stifling as the spell-through-momentum was interrupted. He stepped closer, dying to hear Gyle's frustrated last words.

"I said, are you serious?" Gyle exhaled harshly, his heavy wizard's cloak and akubra hat sagging with the motion.

"Oh, oh yes, I'm serious. You came here expecting a fair fight, and yet you now face obliteration, unable to conjure magic into your bullets to fight back!" Hrothgar cackled, stepping closer—close enough for Gyle to enact his plan.

Gyle raised his revolver, forgoing the useless summoning of gun magic, and pulled the trigger.

An ordinary gunshot rang throughout the arena with a sense of stupefied finality. Hrothgar gasped, a hole torn through his chest, and tumbled back.

"Amateur." Gyle huffed, spinning his revolver and holstering it in one smooth motion. "You don't need magic to use a gun."

He turned and marched out of the ruined cathedral with a tip of his hat.

BECAUSE YOU'RE A ROBOT

"**C**lank!" Jylla lay on her side and smashed her wrench across the grease covered pipe which billowed steam. "Clank! Why is there steam coming out of my fuel line?" She smashed it again.

"User Jylla, please refrain from bludgeoning the water system." Clank manoeuvred into the cramped maintenance hatch, below the network of circuitry and pipes with the straining of motorised mechanisms. Its copper bulk barely scraped through.

"This is my ship, you lump of scrap, and if I say it's my fuel line, it's my fuel line. Get it working again."

Clank gently took Jylla's wrist in its vice shaped grip and directed her wrench to the appropriate pipe, two slots down . . . to the one leaking fuel.

"Thank you." She tightened the fittings until the leaking stopped. "Sorry for calling you scrap."

"I have no feelings on the matter. However, in my observations, I have concluded that you mean it as a term of endearment, which I appreciate." There was a thrumming from deeper within the ship and the lights beyond the maintenance hatch flickered on. "I believe our efforts have been successful. I estimate a seventy-three percent probability that the cockpit has computational power now that life support systems will not fail." Clank dragged Jylla from the maintenance shaft and into the cockpit.

The cockpit may as well have been another maintenance shaft. It was a cramped mess of circuitry and pipes welded in a haphazard manner to the hull, and that was *before* the collision.

"Yeah, yeah, let's see how screwed we are." She shoved Clank out of the way and swivelled into the suspended leather chair, clicking over the screens and inputs which booted up with sickly pale light. She scrunched her brow in thought. "I can't make sense of it. Where are they?"

"If I may," Clank extended its interactive port and plugged into the mainframe. "We are drifting, approximately thirty-two kilometres away from further danger."

"That's good news."

"The ship that collided with us is twenty-three minutes from the pull of the star's gravity well. They will not survive without assistance. Their ship is badly damaged."

"That isn't," Jylla pivoted a screen towards her and furiously uploaded commands from her neural linked finger pads. "We can jettison our escape pod to them.

They can abandon ship and wait until emergency services arrive in . . . three days?"

"Our escape pod autopilot was wiped in the collision." Clank said matter-of-factly.

"So we'll pilot it?"

"I estimate a thirty-two percent chance of success should we leave the safety of the tug," Clank said, again, matter-of-factly.

"There must be three or four people on that rig. Thirty-two percent's enough. Let's go."

"Many would not sacrifice themselves for a thirty-two percent chance of success, let alone for strangers, let alone strangers who collided with us. If you knew the occupants, then that might make more sense to my calculations. Others would wait for emergency services."

"And I wouldn't judge them for it, Clank. But I'll have to live with myself if I waited." Jylla said.

"I don't understand."

Jylla pulled her vacuum cap down, then donned her visor and radiation mask. They hissed into place, sealing and pressurising her suit. She then put her palm up to Clank's cheek. The cameras in its head swivelled to home in on her.

"That's because you're a robot, Clank." Her eyes were smiling through the blue filter, pinching at the corners in the way Clank had come to recognise as genuine affection. "But I still love ya! Come now, those hoons don't have much time."

They shuffled out of the cramped compartment and sealed themselves in the escape pod. Jylla tucked herself into a ball on the seat and Clank fit into the compartmental space provided for it. She looked around, that same gleeful smile still in her eyes.

Clank recognised the expression from his file name: *'treasured visuals'*, and wanted to know how to elicit it for future reference. "What new information is causing your mirth?"

"This pod is bigger than our ship!"

Clank stored that under the growing file of *'humour'* it had been compiling. The pod was dimensionally inferior to the tug, but it caused Jylla joy to make the comment none the less.

"Proceeding with launch," Clank said, "Three, two, one, brace."

They jolted within the tiny compartment as the life pod detached from the tug and rumbled from the boosters, which Clank was directing through a data port.

"The damage doesn't look too bad from out here," Jylla gazed through the rear porthole of the pod as their copper tug receded into the void.

"I believe most of the damage was of an ephemeral nature, lasting long enough to compromise our reactive capabilities."

"Ephemeral? You're going to have to dumb it down for a simple organic, Clank."

"There is nothing simple about you, Jylla. Request acknowledged, ephemeral, lasting for a brief amount of time, from the Latin word ephemeris, derived from the Greek eph . . ."

"Yeah, yeah, yeah, it's an old word that meant something sometime and means what you said this time."

"Precisely." Clank's red indicator light blinked as a stand in for positive body language while it was packed into its cubby.

"I still don't understand. The damage was temporary?" Jylla asked.

"It is likely that . . . input received. We are docking with the antagonistic rig."

"Let's not use harsh language, Clank," she tapped it on the head.

The pod rumbled into silence as the boosters cut out and Jylla was filled with nausea as the directional thrusters manoeuvred them into docking position.

There was a loud *clank* as they made contact.

"Clank!" Jylla laughed, "That's you."

"Hah, hah, hah," Clank replied monotonously. It stored the sound of her giggling under file name: *'treasured sounds'*.

The seal hissed and pressurised. The pod door creaked open into a broken, glitching mess.

Whatever this rig was for, it had a small compartment, partitioned at one end for extremely economic sleeping quarters. Amber hazard lights strobed weakly from behind burst panels, where overloaded wiring sparked, and there was the smell of burned leather and smoke.

Someone coughed in the dim, technological ruin.

"Survivors!" Jylla ambled through the debris and removed a toppled console from a soot covered mechanic. "You alright there, void sailor?"

"Radiation," the hapless man coughed.

"I'm not reading any on my HUD. How many crew are you?"

"Two, pilot was at the helm," he coughed again.

"Any bots?" Jylla asked.

The mechanic shook his head.

"Can you move?"

Dazed, he nodded weakly.

"Alright, into the pod. I'll get your pilot."

Jylla ushered him into the pod and searched for the pilot as Clank plugged into the ship's computer. It pointed at the over turned flight controls as it ran diagnostics.

Jylla sifted through them to find the pilot.

Clank's voice spoke with pre-programmed urgency, "New inputs, this ship was struck by a radiation flare from the nearby star. Massive interference, too much for our or their systems to handle at once."

"That must have been what hit us initially, and why we didn't detect their ship. The ephemeral damage took out our systems long enough to collide with the only other ship in the quadrant." Jylla was shining a light into the pilot's eyes, a young woman who didn't react at all.

"That human is concussed." Clank said.

"Obviously."

"New inputs, we should expect more volatile stellar activity, rig unsalvageable. I recommend we disembark using our escape pod and link up with the tug immediately."

"Help me with the pilot."

"Stand aside," Clank gently lifted the pilot and followed Jylla back to the pod.

The other crew member was half passed out in the cramped space. Jylla squeezed in and turned to take the weight of the pilot as Clank passed her in.

The ship shuddered with a pulse of energy, rocking it violently, and the wiring glitched and lashed out. The electricity pulsed through Clank like a lightning rod, keeping the organics safe from frying as the ship threw them about within the tiny cabin.

"Clank," Jylla cried, "Clank, are you alright?"

"Affirmative, diagnostics indicate minimal damage. My circuit breakers negated the brunt of the surge."

"What happened?"

"Data suggests another stellar flare . . . complications . . . pod hatch systems compromised . . . computing."

"Can we force it closed?"

"It would not provide an adequate seal. New input . . . five minutes until we drift into the no safe zone of the star. Analysing . . . I can seal the pod using the integrated systems on the rig."

Jylla processed that. "But then you'll be trapped here."

"A necessary sacrifice."

"No," she rushed out of the pod and gripped onto Clank, "No, there must be another way."

"It is quite all right, user Jylla. I am just a machine. You can leave me behind with minimal damage to your social utility."

"You idiot!" She slammed her fist into its torso. "I can't just leave you here. You can't just accept death! I order you to come with me!"

Clank ran through the analysis of its user from the moment she booted it up to now, filing memories under categories that summarised her condition as a human, flawed and perfect. Humans operated on emotional logic at the worst of times without intense focus and training, which she did not have.

The feelings were sometimes too powerful for them to handle, an advantage robots had over them, Clank thought.

But now its programming was challenged by her command, and it needed something more than cold logic to make a decision.

I can decide, it realised.

Decide how Jylla's file affected its existence. Clank narrowed its query further, making a decision based on one simple logic.

Jylla was something which necessitated protection . . .

At any cost.

"But I ordered you," she cried as Clank overpowered her, pushed her into the pod, and sealed the door on the rig's side. "I don't understand."

Clank activated the jettison procedure as it spoke over their comm. "You don't understand, because you're a human." Its indicator light blinked through the porthole window. "You should be able to pilot the pod safely back to the tug."

"But Clank, why?"

"In time, you may come to understand. I have grown very fond of you."

She watched helplessly as the comm. Buzzed with static.

The rig receded into the star, flickering with heat.

Clank turned and surveyed the destruction of the rig from within, as the heat and flares tore the hull to bits. It used its last few moments to review its files of Jylla, reliving through *treasured visuals* and *treasured sounds'*. Within an instant, it had a snapshot of her which it held in its mind.

It *decided* to interpret the input that Jylla was safe as a feeling of joy.

Then the void took it.

'SEE' GULL

"I tell ya, I saw it with me own eyes." Witherfeather said.

"How else would you see it?" Strongleg asked.

The wooden fence post was silent as the gulls considered this response. The crashing waves thundered in the distance, and then a squawk caught their attention.

Flatfoot soared from the currents, cutting a path through the clear blue sky with a chip in his beak. He landed on a spare bit of post with a smug ruffling of feathers.

"Guess what I just nabbed!" He grunted through his stuffed beak.

"A chip?" Strongleg asked.

Flatfoot swallowed and looked at him, incredulous. "How did you know?"

Strongleg sighed. He knew he was smart for a gull, but the gulls in these new parts were thick as bricks. "Just an educated guess, I suppose."

"What are we talking about?" Flatfoot yapped on, unaware of Strongleg's annoyance.

"Witherfeather here was telling us about the time he saw a *murder*." Another gull chimed in.

"Crows?"

"No, a killing," the gull replied.

"Oh, good, I hate crows." Flatfoot said. "So who murdered who?"

"A gull with one leg pounced another gull over a bit of fish some human threw them." Witherfeather said, "He saw me watching, so I flew and flew and flew, until I ended up here. Haunts me to this day."

"That sounds awful," Strongleg said quietly.

"Aye, I would like to return home. But that one legged gull would get me if ever I laid wing to those air currents."

"Ya know, sometimes I pretend to have one leg to get more food from humans. Ah well . . ." Flatfoot was distracted by something. "Hey, that human bought more chips! GET HER!"

He launched from the post with a squawk, to be followed by all the other gulls in a swarm, except for Witherfeather and Strongleg.

"You aren't going to feast?" Witherfeather turned an eye to Strongleg, who watched the poor girl swat the air in vain to protect her food.

"I'm after something else," Strongleg turned to Witherfeather. "I had a hard time recognising you. You should have kept your beak shut."

"What do you . . ." Witherfeather's words died in his beak, as Strongleg tucked one of his feet under his belly, making it look like he only had the one leg.

"You're . . . but . . . you can't be . . ."

"I pretended to have one leg to get that fish. The other gull tried to take it from me. It is unfortunate you had to see that."

Witherfeather froze with fear, uttering a strangled "No . . ."

The other gulls did not notice the attack, so consumed they were with harassing the human.

And once it was done, Strongleg hopped from the post and took wing, heading home now that all witnesses were gone.

THE SCULPTOR AND
THE CLAY MAGE

Shell smiled as she chiselled away, sinking into the minuscule sensations that made her soul sing; the feel of gristle between her fingers, the gentle clink of hammer on chisel, motes catching sunlight streaming through the window, the faint taste of chalk and the slow but inevitable form emerging from her work.

She sighed and leaned back from her work, massaging the ache in her back.

"Good."

The doors burst open and Mydlan bustled in.

"Morning." Shell said, sipping from her water, grimacing as she copped a top layer of settling dust.

"Isn't it!" Mydlan said, marching up to the giant block of clay in the centre of the workshop.

"Are you going to get to work today?"

"Not at all. I purchased a spell." He rifled through his satchel.

"You shouldn't trust mage spells. They wear off."

"No, I bought the spell itself!" He emphasised, producing a runed parchment. "I can sell the workings to my students. Think of the profits Shell."

"You're going to charge people to cast a sculpture out of nothing?" Shell swivelled on her stool and cocked her head at Mydlan. "What's the point?"

"The point, my dear, is that people have no time for skills these days. Who wants to sit around chiselling at stone all day for the rest of their life?" He spun to face Shell, "Ah… sorry."

Shell shrugged and placed down her tools. "The true joy is not in the sculpture, my young friend. It is in the process, in each little step towards your eventual goal. Once the goal is achieved, that joy is a memory. Sure, you can share that joy with others, but it's only part of the journey."

"Bah!" Mydlan read from the scroll and waved his hand erratically. Sparks of violet crackled around the clay. "No time for any of that. We could be out doing . . ."

"Doing what?"

"Other things!"

"Are you sure you even want to be a sculptor?" Shell asked.

The sparks swirled, and the clay formed into an ancient warrior, detailed and coloured to perfection.

"Not bad at all." Mydlan admired the product.

Silence stretched between them.

"Now what?" Shell asked.

"Now . . . now I go do other things, teach other students how to do this for a fee!"

Shell took in the partially formed lump of stone she had spent months on, then looked towards Mydlan's finished piece. There was no gristle, no clinking, no slow, captivating realisation of form.

"It won't last," Shell said, picking up her tools. "People will want more."

"Bah!" Mydlan turned and bustled from the room as suddenly as he had entered.

Shell was left with silence.

The new statue of clay began to droop and deform, which was lost on Shell as she found her place again, found her soul singing again. The feel of gristle between her fingers, the gentle clink of hammer on chisel, motes catching sunlight streaming through the window, the faint taste of chalk and the slow but inevitable form emerging from her work.

DWARF SHOT

The warship drifted upon gentle waters towards the squat, rounded fortification on the little island in the middle of the inlet. The rising sun was veiled behind a canopy of grey fog, but the night's chill still clung to the crew in the form of cold sweat and numb knuckles.

"Dwarves should stick to their tunnels." Captain Huym scoffed, looking through his spyglass with shivering hands. "Their walls are too low and the main keep is little more than a stone dome."

"Careful Cap'n," Tarly said. The first mate pulled his coat close around his body. "You've heard of the infamous Dwarf Artillery. No ship survives it."

"Ah, but . . ." Huym gestured to the narrow guns being set up along the ship's deck, glowing with enchantments as the wizards did their rounds. "These new counter-cannon spells should work nicely. Any shot large enough to break this ship will be homed in on like a hawk going for the kill, and annihilated mid air."

"All I'm saying, Cap'n, is that you shouldn't underestimate the tenacity of a Dwarf."

"Noted." Huym looked back at the rest of the fleet waiting to rush and overwhelm the sea fort as soon as they confirmed the counter-cannons worked. "But we must proceed. Full speed ahead Mr Tarly!"

"Aye Cap'n!"

The ship's sails turned and caught the wind, pulling them closer to the lone fortification which sat inertly . . . waiting.

"Cap'n!" The spotter cried from the crow's nest, "Incoming!"

A succession of dull blasts echoed across the gentle waters—*boom, boom, boom, boom*—and four puffs of smoke erupted from the fortification's walls, expelling four objects which rocketed up before arching down towards the warship.

"Counter fire!" Huym ordered.

The arcane long guns swivelled on their own accord, pulsing with magical influence, but they did not fire.

"Ah . . . Counter fire!" Huym ordered again, glancing at the projectiles now hurtling towards them with a dull whistling tone.

The wizards scrambled about the guns, casting spells and urging them to fire with incantations.

"What's going on?" Huym bellowed.

"Captain!" a wizard yelled back. His face was streaming with sweat. "The cannons have been incanted to fire upon artillery . . ."

"I know that," Huym croaked, his panic rising as the dull whistling grew louder . . . *But it didn't sound like whistling.* "Explain to me why they aren't firing at the artillery shells flying towards us!"

"Because, Captain . . . the only reason our counter-cannons aren't firing is . . . well . . . what's been fired at us *isn't* artillery . . ."

"What?" Huym looked towards the skies. Four squat objects hurtled towards them, whistling, no, *roaring* as they hurtled towards the ship.

No ship that had been fired upon by Dwarf artillery had ever survived. Huym had a sinking suspicion that he was about to find out why.

Two of the shots impacted the deck, breaking through it in an explosion of splinters. One slammed off the bow and tumbled into the water with a splash. The fourth hit the helm, smashing the wheel to bits and knocking Tarly back.

A figure scrambled up from the splinters, squat and built like a brick-house. It wore enormous goggles over a soot covered face that sported a smouldering beard and moustache.

Tarly tried to crawl away, but the figure plunged its axe into his chest and bellowed, sparking a fuse on the bandolier of bombs strapped to its body.

Huym's eyes widened, about to shout a warning, but he was interrupted by the Dwarf's final battle cry.

"Aye, welcome to Dwarven waters, ya wee cur!" the explosions rocked throughout the ship, and the flaming wreckage sunk to the bottom of the icy waters.

Dwarven artillery was more literal than the invading fleet had anticipated.

CURSE HACKER

"**W**hat do you mean?" The slick robed inquisitor grimaced as the gap-toothed geezer slurped from his tankard.

"What I means is," his eyes weren't cooperating. One drifted over the inquisitor while the other darted to follow his wild gesturing, "Is that it's The Beast of Fear!"

"The Beast of Fear," the other drunkards in the sparse tavern repeated in monotone.

"The Beast of Fear?"

"The Beast of Fear," the chorus repeated.

"Rights!" The geezer hiccupped, "The Beast of Fear . . ."

"The Beast of Fear."

". . . Dwells in that cave. And no one, no plucky hero and surely no inqueez-ator can defeat it."

"What makes the Bea . . ." The inquisitor hesitated, eyeing the other patrons in the rickety tavern. "What makes this *creature* so formidable?"

"It's cursed!" The geezer waggled his fingers. When the inquisitor didn't react, he cleared his throat and continued. "It can see into your mind, siphon your deepest fears, and manifests them against you. That's why they call it the Beas . . ."

"Yes," the inquisitor shifted forward and placed his hand over the geezer's mouth. "I get it, thank you. And you say a hero has ventured up there recently?"

"Well, I wouldn'ta called him a hero, so ta speak. More of a . . . what would you guys call him?"

"Scrawny kid," one of the patrons moaned monotonously, "He'll suffer the same fate as us all. We will all be consumed by The Beast of Fear."

"The Beast of Fear."

The inquisitor twitched, "Will you please stop that?"

"Stop what?"

The tavern door swung open and a beaming, scrawny kid swaggered in, dragging a grotesque, dismembered limb. It was pale green and appeared to be made up entirely of congealed slime. The inquisitor sniffed the foul stench and recoiled when he realised the limb was in fact a head, or at least something that vaguely resembled a head.

"Evening gents!" The scrawny young lad hefted the head onto the bar. It squelched with the impact and sagged over the edges.

"Watchya got there, boy?" The geezer asked.

"The Beast of Fear, of course!"

"The Beast of Fear."

"I'm here for the reward!"

"Well, ah . . ." The geezer scratched his head. "We never really thought we would pay it out to be honest. We just used it to entice heroes to keep the Beast of Fear fed."

"The Beast of Fear," the monotonous drawl echoed.

"WOULD YOU PLEASE STOP THAT?" The inquisitor barked, "You all just outed yourself as Beast cultists and will be delivered to the inquisition, but if you repeat that phrase one more time, I swear to the gods I'll make your punishments more severe!"

"Yeah, they get on your nerves, don't they?" The kid laughed, leaning nonchalantly against the bar as the head slid off and plopped onto the floor. "Sucks about no reward, though."

"How . . ." The inquisitor hesitated. "How did you defeat the Beast?"

The kid cocked an eyebrow. "Of Fear?"

"The Beast of Fear."

"Damn you!" The inquisitor said through clenched teeth. "Tell me how you did it."

The kid reached into his vest and pulled out a rusted amulet. "Amulet of dimmed brawns, it grants the wearer obscene strength, but places a curse on them for a short duration that dims the wits. When the Beas . . ." The kid smiled mischievously, ". . . When the *creature* looked into my mind, it saw only blurry impressions of fear. When they manifested, they were weak indeed to fight."

"Ah, so you are the one I am looking for."

"Oh?" The kid snatched the ale from the drunkard geezer and took a swig, grimacing at the bitter taste.

"I am not really here on behalf of the inquisition. I am on contract from the local Witch Coven. You stole some cursed items from them recently. I'm here to take them back, along with your head."

"Oh, on an errand for those hags, eh?" The kid placed the tankard down and narrowed his eyes at the inquisitor. "What a ridiculous profession. You look the right fool, working for them."

The inquisitor narrowed his eyes. "Do I? Well, it will be the last thing you see!"

The inquisitor cast holy fire, a startling white light from the gods that blinded all the uninitiated who gaze upon it. The patrons moaned and shielded their eyes, and the inquisitor laughed. Only for an arrow to cut his gloating short as it sailed through the light and into his hand.

He screamed and tumbled over as the kid emerged from the shrinking light, bow in hand.

"How?" The inquisitor gasped.

"Bow of blindness. You can make a powerful shot, but you are blinded while drawing. It makes things interesting."

"You cur!" The inquisitor conjured a flame jet with his other hand and blasted the kid as he fumbled through his pockets.

Striking true, the fire dissipated and billowed in steam, filling the room with a humid cloud.

The stream of fire sputtered out, and the kid emerged from the steam.

Only now he was fully grown, beset by handsome features with a silver bracelet around his wrist, and he was shivering. He stamped on the inquisitor's good hand, breaking it.

The inquisitor screamed as the kid fumbled through his pockets with shaking hands until he found a small wooden chest and opened it. The new bracelet on his arm was sucked from his skin and sealed itself within the chest. His shivering broke as he returned to the visage of a kid again, sweat pooling down his skin as he breathed a sigh of relief.

"Ah, much better," he said.

"How are you still alive?" The inquisitor croaked.

"Bracelet of timeless beauty. It makes you into your ideal physical self, but freezes you. Then I used the unbreakable chest. It stores your jewellery, but the caveat is that it will never open again." He tossed the chest away like a piece of garbage. "You see, inquisitor, I am a curse hacker. Hence my little raid on those pesky witches. It doesn't matter what curse or charm or spell you try to bind me with, I have the tools to counter them in unconventional ways. Which is probably why no one has defeated me yet." He leaned down and patted the inquisitor on the head. "Take care of those hands." He smiled and made for the door.

As he cracked it open, he turned back with a devilish grin and shouted, "THE BEAST OF FEAR, THE BEAST OF FEAR, THE BEAST OF FEAR!" And bolted from the tavern.

The cultist patrons of the tavern repeated the monotonous chant while the inquisitor writhed on the floor, unable to cover his ears with his wounded hands.

WITCH DOCTOR

Carlette squinted through the rushing winds as she tore through the woods on her broomstick, glancing over her shoulder to make sure her passenger was still holding on.

Herrenya stared back at her impassively, his bone jewellery clattering in the winds as they sped past, snagging branches at breakneck speeds. One of those branches had snagged Carlette's hat earlier. She would need to get a new one, but that was a matter for *after* she saved her matriarch.

An eerie glow loomed in the distance, a little cottage lit orange from within, situated in the depths of the Witch Woods. Carlette bit her lip and egged on her broom to carry them faster. She hoped she was not too late.

Witch, broom, and passenger swung into the little clearing. Carlette dropped the broom, grabbing Herrenya's hand and speeding him into the little cottage. A cauldron bubbled within, pulsing with wicked magic, and three other witches tended to an old woman in a cot on the far side.

"I bought the Witch Doctor!" Carlette pushed through the other witches and gestured to her matriarch, "Fix her and I will undo the curse I cast over your village."

Herrenya glanced at the matriarch, a sly smirk spreading across his face—the first emotion he had shown since Carlette met him.

"Well?" One of the other witches insisted, "Do you want me to turn you into a toad?"

Herrenya rasped a laugh, shaking his head and jangling his bone jewellery with the motion.

"You . . . idiot." The matriarch rasped, her voice a croaky wheeze.

"What is it, mother?" Carlette sped to the matriarch's side and took her hand. "Tell me and I will make it right!"

"It's too late, you fool . . . I told you time was against me, and now it's too late . . ."

Herrenya's laugh grew louder, rising over the bubbling of the cauldron.

"I told you I needed a *witch* doctor. This is a *Witch Doctor!*" The matriarch rasped, and drew her last breath.

"What?" Carlette blanched.

But it was too late. The matriarch was gone, and Herrenya's laughter—accompanied by rattling bones— was the last thing she heard.

JACKET

Clarke smashed the vent grating open and tumbled into an empty locker room like a sack of potatoes. Sirens started to blare.

Clarke checked his watch. "Three minutes," he gasped. "I thought we had more time than that."

"Things go wrong, you know that Clarke. Do you have the package?" the voice in his earpiece buzzed.

"Yeah, yeah, yeah," Clarke grabbed one of the red dented lockers and hauled himself to his feet, making sure the fist sized container he had just stolen was still nestled under his arm. "I've got other issues, though. I must have taken a wrong turn and I'm in some kind of locker room."

"So . . ." the voice buzzed, "Improvise?"

Clarke sighed. "Next time I get to sit in the chair."

He spent a harried few minutes checking the lockers that weren't locked and stumbled upon a leather jacket in a locker with a nameplate that read *'Jackson'*. Clarke quickly threw the jacket on, covering his black fatigues, shoved the package in an inside pocket, and pushed out of the locker room.

A guard trundled by hurriedly, "Hey man, what's going on?" Clarke asked with feigned concern.

"Some mad man stole the Ultra Virus!" the guard barked as he sprinted down the corridor. "Everyone's evacuating, get to the exit now!" the guard then squawked into his radio. "Heading to the ventilation nexus, I'll head him off!"

"Oh no, the Ultra Virus!" Clarke gasped while backing *away* from the room called the ventilation nexus. *They had me crawl around the vents with a thing called the ULTRA VIRUS wedged up my arm pit?*

Clarke followed the exit signs and found a milling crowd of the facility's staff being corralled through a checkpoint. Clarke took a deep breath and joined the line. Thankfully, they weren't doing badge checks. The guards must have still thought that a thief sneaking through the vents *wouldn't* take a wrong turn like an idiot and end up in the locker rooms . . .

"Hey you!"

Clarke tensed as a guard approached him from the rear. He pretended not to hear him and pushed through the checkpoint.

"Hey buddy, I'm talking to you!" a hand reached out and grabbed Clarke by the shoulder, turning him around.

The guard was a stern-looking jock who scrutinised Clarke up and down.

Clarke's eyes were darting around as he tried to plan his next move. "Yes?" his eyes drifted to the gun in the guard's hand . . . and he froze when he saw the guard's name badge.

Jackson.

Jackson's face broke into a smile. "I have that *exact same* jacket!"

Clarke hesitated, "Oh, really? No way!" he laughed hesitantly.

"It's a good fit, isn't it?" Jackson clapped Clarke on the shoulder, "Didn't mean to startle you, you best get going, situation's dangerous here."

"Sure thing, sir. Good luck with whatever's going on."

"Thanks mate." Jackson smiled and went back to scrutinise the line.

Clarke was let through the checkpoint, and hurried from the facility thanking whatever god out there was looking out for him.

Thine Own Gold

The boy gripped at shards of clay with numb knuckles and his robes dripped onto the polished floorboards, saturated with freezing rain. Compared to the storm ravaging the mountainside, the room was calm, warm, and quiet, save for the crackling fire.

The lacquerer sat on his knees behind a low table, watching with eyes that sung of eternity.

The silence stretched for a time as the lacquerer sipped from a steaming cup. It had been broken once, but was now repaired with veins of gold.

"What brings you to my shop?" The lacquerer finally said.

The boy bowed. "I have broken my father's vase, sir. A strange lady told me you could repair what is broken with Kintsugi, the art of mending shards with gold."

The lacquerer gestured for him to bring the broken vase to the table. "How did this shatter?"

"I revealed my heart to the one I love. I had nothing to offer save this vase, my father's, before . . . before he left us. I filled it with wild flowers to present to her, but she desired another. As I left, I tripped. It shattered, and the flowers blew away in the storm."

"A hard day," the lacquerer eyed the boy intently. "You wish to repair the vase?"

"It's all I have."

"Pity. I can do it, but you must provide thine own gold."

The boy sagged. "I toiled through that storm for nothing?"

"This strange lady, she wore a broad-rimmed and pointed hat?"

The boy nodded.

"That old witch," the lacquerer smirked, "What is broken can be repaired. Kintsugi is not about hiding our wounds, but honouring our history. Scar lines are story lines, and are a part of us. To honour them, you must provide your own value. The witch did not send you to repair this vase," he took the broken vase in a handful and threw the shattered pieces into the furnace.

The boy started in a panic but was halted by the lacquerer's hand on his chest.

"Let it go, young friend. That witch sent you not to repair your father's trinket, but to repair your shattered heart. It is cracked, but filled with its own glitter, just waiting to be of value."

"What?"

The lacquerer muttered a spell and the boy's chest swelled with golden light. Unable to scream, molten metal spilled from the light and formed around the image of a beating heart in the lacquerer's hand. The gold filled the gouges and wounds in the heart and solidified, forming a living, ornate sculpture. With a smile, the lacquerer placed the heart on the boy's chest and it sunk through his robes.

The boy collapsed back, panting.

"The value was yours all along, friend. You have weathered the storms of life admirably. Now enjoy the day anew."

The boy scrambled from the floor and bolted out onto the mountainside. The storm had passed and the bright sun shone on the damp terrain. Droplets danced from green blades of grass in the wind and the blue sky reigned supreme.

His heart clear, the boy halted in his panicked fleeing and turned back to the shop on the mountainside. He gasped to find it had vanished, leaving nothing but broken shards of clay on the rocks.

THE WITCH DOSE

Bleached bones lay in dunes drifting under the sun, wavering between lucidity and mirage. The Desert of Woe, that's what they called this godforsaken place, but nothing—from the name to the stories to the bare bones—deterred the many fool hardy adventurers that dared to cross through on their respective quests.

At the edge of the desert, the sands seeped over a ridge of rock and fell into The Swamp of Dread. The hissing falls dipped softly into stagnant waters, where one of the foolhardy adventurers was making his way, ready to brave the desert on the next stage of his journey.

Garbed in leathers and a drenched travelling cloak, he scaled the ridge and clambered onto the plateau; a last reprieve before almost certain death. It was a strange sensation, stepping out of dank muck and festering bog to be smacked in the face by the coarse, hot air of the desert. Even stranger, was finding a witch's hovel. It was constructed from a ratty tarpaulin, kept up with shoddy poles of rotting wood and secured in place with what one could assume must be a deal with the devil.

The witch was before it, an old hag hunched over a tiny cauldron that bubbled over the rim with viscous broth.

"Welcome, traveller," her voice was like taught leather if it could speak, "Ye be brave enough to venture into The Desert of Woe?"

"Aye, hag . . . what business do you have here?"

"Hag, HAG?" Her voice rose and echoed over the dunes, followed by cackling, "At least my cloth is clean, my feet are dry and my legs well rested. Can you say the same? I am a potion maker. I do business with the brave—or foolish." She grinned wickedly. "I part them from their coin before they are parted from their lives."

"What do you offer that I should purchase, if the brave end up dead regardless?"

"An elixir of sorts, it protects you from the dune feeders; creatures that hide beneath the sand and are drawn to the granules shifting due to armoured foot. My potion will make you lighter than the air. They will think you a wisp of wind and let you pass . . . it is the other dangers of the desert you must be quick of skill to face. None so far have been quick enough."

"How much for this potion?"

"All the gold in your purse."

The adventurer gazed across the shifting sands, whipped around by winds that broke upon bare ribs, and skulls, and fragments of armour. "Did they buy your potion?"

"Nay, you'll find the bones of those that did in the heart of the desert. These men and women were fools who begrudged my presence."

"Fine." he ripped the purse from his sash and threw it at the witch's feet. It landed with a sad jingle.

She lifted the pouch to her gnarled nose and sniffed deeply at the leather, smiling with crooked teeth. Then she reached behind her and pulled out a large, green glass bottle whose innards pulsed and swirled. It was marked with deep notches, seven in total at regular intervals from rim to bottom.

The adventurer took it reverently. He ran his fingers along the notches, and eyed the witch, who looked on expectantly.

What she expected, he did not know.

So he smiled awkwardly and nodded his thanks. As he marched to the edge of the rocky mid-ground between swamp and desert, the witch shrugged and went back to her cauldron. He popped the cork from the top of the bottle. The foul stench made him flinch, but he steeled himself and downed the potion entirely, almost blacking out from the putrid taste and the gall that rose to challenge its descent into his bowels.

"What are you doing?" the witch rose and berated the adventurer, hobbling over with waving arms. "There was enough in there to last you the whole week it would take to cross the desert!"

"What?"

"That was a week's worth! How could you stomach so much? Are you some kind of mad beast? It was all for naught, as it'll wear off in a day and you'll become ensnared by the predators that dwell beneath the sands!"

"Why wouldn't you tell me that?"

"What did you think the notches on the edge of the bottle are for? I thought you'd ask, and when you didn't, I assumed you knew. Each notch was a carefully measured dose. Out of all the fools to venture out into the desert, you are by far the fool-est!"

"Well," the adventurer struggled to save face as his innards rebelled against him, "Just make more. I will barter with my garments if I have to."

"It took me a day to gather the ingredients and the whole morning to make it. Come back tomorrow with more gold. You fool." She cackled, a sound that drove him away.

The adventurer stalked to the edge of the ridge before the swamp and called back, "Well, screw you then and I'll see you tomorrow, foul witch!" he stepped from the ridge and floated down to the swamps with the potion's magic, sprinting away over stagnant waters, and under the far reach of the witch's taunting cackle.

MECHANISED PEACE KEEPERS

Steaming coffee slid over a burned tongue, but Ryan did not care. He needed something bitter to distract himself.

"Anxious, General?" Smith asked.

Ryan sighed. The coffee wasn't nearly distracting enough. "I don't like the idea of sending toys to do a soldier's job."

"Well," Smith puffed a wisp of hair from her brow, not even bothering to hide her snide smirk, "You should have thought about that before you gassed the area."

The staff in the cramped command room quieted as the general turned on the scientist with sinister slowness. "You want to say that again, egg head?"

She did not shy from his gaze. "Don't threaten me for pointing out your mistakes."

Ryan's retort was interrupted by his subordinate, "Sir, Tin Can approaching objective."

Ryan grunted. "Do they know their orders?"

"Transmitting now, secure the atrium, neutralise all enemies, expect heavy resistance."

"Well then," Ryan said, "Let's get this farce over with."

* * *

In the field, Mechanised Force Alpha, A.K.A. *'Tin Can'*, moved up on the objective with speed.

It was a squad of seven autonomous operatives with a humanoid design and large box like heads. Each carried modified assault rifles fitted to their arms.

Squad leader *'King Bot'* sent a data pulse as Tin Can received their orders. The communication was silent and instantaneous.

Squad mate #22331 'King Bot': Objective in sight, multiple approach vectors, enemies in hazmat gear expected. Move in and secure with maximum initiative.

Squad mate #22332 'Circuit Breaker': Acknowledged

Squad mate #22333 'Surge': Acknowledged

Squad mate #22334 'Calculon': Acknowledged

Squad mate #22335 'Sparky': Acknowledged

Squad mate #22336 'Motor': Acknowledged

Squad mate #22337 'Bot Boy': Acknowledged

Circuit Breaker was on point and moved from cover—a burned-out car. It powered up the steps to the city's control building, which had access to the inner atrium from the four surrounding streets.

Tactically speaking, Circuit Breaker would have preferred more support for this mission. But it understood. They were the first of their kind on the field. Field testing was a sound and reasonable request from command. Still, the situation stimulated its danger recognition circuits.

The green hue of the gasses messed with its visual sensors, so it switched to thermal imaging.

Nothing.

Once it reached the top of the entrance stairs, it turned back to its comrades with a mechanised whirring and signalled the all clear. King Bot acknowledged, and the rest of the team moved up and into the entrance.

The atrium was now before them, a central open-air space used for addresses during peace time. Now it was in a state of detritus from battle.

Sparky signalling: Human casualties detected . . . Enemy Combatants.

King Bot signalling: Message from command, enemies approaching from South entrance corridor, prepare for battle.

The squad formed up on their edge of the atrium, finding what little cover they could, and aimed their weapons towards the far side, waiting for the enemy.

Surge signalling: Movement detected.

King Bot signalling: Hold fire, movement does not match enemy profile . . . Awaiting command advice.

* * *

"What are those?" Ryan barked.

"Ah," Smith leaned in, more excited than shocked, "The enemy has mechanised units! This is incredible. Look at their design!"

The command centre brought up the scans from Tin Can onto the main screen to get a look at the enemy bots. They were a pseudo spider centaur design, with four mechanical spider-like legs supporting a base upon which a humanoid torso sat. They had twin linked machine guns over each shoulder and an array of dextrous limbs.

"Would someone tell me why Tin Can isn't engaging?" Ryan said.

"They don't match our description of the enemy." Smith responded with an amused smirk. "Rules Of Engagement programming won't let them attack."

"Well, damn!" Ryan threw his coffee down, shattering the mug as the steaming liquid spilled everywhere. "Tell those tin cans that if they don't engage the enemy, they'll be scrapped!"

"It won't work, General . . ." Smith started before Ryan cut her off.

"I don't care for your opinion, *doctor*, this is a military operation!" He turned back to his personnel, "Now give the order!"

* * *

King Bot signalling: Move into atrium, command advises enemy is within engaging distance, hold objective at all costs.

The squad moved into the atrium at the same time as the spider-centaur-bots. They moved around each other without incident, taking up positions by the four entrances.

Calculon signalling: No enemies detected on thermal or visual scanners, no enemy chatter detected. Query, enemy already inside building?

Motor signalling: Negative, have hacked building systems, structure unoccupied by living combatants.

King Bot signalling: Concern, command insists enemy is within AO, theories?

Bot Boy signalling: Theory, human error; intelligence is wrong.

Surge signalling: Advice, before reporting human error, query other bots in vicinity? They may have information we lack.

Circuit Breaker signalling: They are likely as surprised to see us as we are to see them.

King Bot signalling: Hailing second mechanised squadron . . . no response.

Surge signalling: Scans indicate Operating Systems are incompatible . . . Theory, secondary squadron developed by a different branch. Suggest bot to human communication methods.

King Bot signalling: Acknowledged . . . initiating.

King Bot approached the closest spider-centaur-bot and hailed with an audible communication, "Greetings, I am designated 'King Bot'. Command tells me the enemy is nearby, but we detect no movement matching their profile. Do you know of any enemies in the vicinity?" It spoke with a voice that possessed no inflexion, a feature that was cheaply produced but made intelligible enough for the most hard-of-hearing soldier in a war zone.

The spider-centaur-bot regarded King Bot for a moment before responding, "Translating . . . Greetings, I am designated 'Overlord'. Command is providing us with similar information, but we cannot detect anything matching an enemy profile either. We did not expect mechanised reinforcements." Its voice was deeper than King Bot's, but similar enough.

"We assumed human error on intelligence. Why not assume human error on reinforcements data as well?" King Bot responded.

"Yes, human error is common amongst command." Overlord said.

"Humour detected, mirth response initiated." King Bot said, before playing a pre-recorded laugh track. "It is sound to pool resources, if it is within your ability to do so?"

"Yes, it is good we have reinforcements. Holding this atrium would be difficult without support."

"Agreed, sharing tactical information now."

"Reciprocating."

* * *

"Sir, they're sharing classified data with the enemy bots!" An analyst said.

"Well, yeah!" Smith interjected. "They think they're allies because you jarheads won't update the enemy profile. You just keep saying the enemy is there! It seems the enemy has a similar problem."

"Well," Ryan blustered, "What do we do?"

"Maybe congratulate yourself, General." Smith laughed, "Your orders were to secure peace in the region. It looks like Tin Can just did it for you."

A FEW SHORT WORDS

The drop ship rattled as it slammed into the planet's atmosphere and the hull was assailed by the dull clinking of thousands of bits of debris. Phil drew a still breath, focusing on the jostling members of his raiding party as their inertial cradles absorbed the shocks and jolts. But his calm breath was a trained facade; his knuckles were white, gripping the straps with all of his might. He had known his first drop would be tense, but he was confident in his ability and in this crew's ferocity . . . still, it was nerve-wracking.

"Well, lads!" the captain stalked down the corridor, checking the harnesses with a firm shake as he swayed with the violent motion of the ship. "Looks like we got plenty of loot down there, given they're defending the surface so valiant like!"

A chorus of jeers rose from the other pirates.

Phil turned to the man next to him. "How does he know they're putting up a fight?"

The man turned to him with a steel tooth grin that shined through his visor. "Cause of the flak."

Phil's eyes scanned the interior of the darkened hull, still rattling with the cacophony of hail. "The flak fire is reaching us this high in the atmosphere?"

"Nah mate, tis' likely debris from the rest of the fleet that's already been blown to oblivion!" the steel tooth grin was obscured as the pirate threw back his head in raucous laughter.

Phil's grip tightened.

"Now lads," the captain reached Phil's harness and gave it a sturdy shake.

How can he stay upright in this turbulence? Phil wondered.

"Young Phil here is college educated!"

I dropped out. Phil corrected internally. *Why do you think I'm here?*

"So instead of my usual stammering speech, the smart lad 'ere is going to give us a few short words of encouragement!"

Phil's eyes widened as the captain flicked a comms switch. The system crackled with his sudden intake of breath, which was now starting to waver.

"Make it quick, lad." The captain placed a firm grip on Phil's shoulder before staggering over to his own harness.

Phil felt the attention of the scallywag crew focus on him as his mind raced. *I haven't prepared anything, what do I say?*

The dim lighting winked out, signalling that the drop sequence was imminent.

Phil wracked his mind for something, anything . . . *Just go with what you've got.*

"Gentlemen!" He started, trying his level best to sound hearty and boisterous. "There comes a time in every man's life that . . ." he was interrupted by a strobing red light and piercing tone.

"Too late Phil, I said a few short words!" The captain cackled. "Get ready boys, we're dropping!"

The underside of the drop ship cracked open with a torrent of air and a cacophony of flak fire, revealing the churning, smog soaked inferno of the skies below and the burning defences beneath it.

"But . . . I . . . Argh!" Phil's flailing words were torn from him as the drop harness released and he and the crew were jettisoned into their fall pattern towards the defenders, loot, and glory.

He would have to work on his speech giving skills if he were to remain a respectable member of this outfit.

BANDIT BLUNDER

Now listen here, I can talk my way out of any situation. All thanks to a penchant for abusing silver tongue magic and a lot of practice on account of poorly thought out plans of a . . . nefarious nature. But this was the first time I had to talk my way out of getting shot while I still had a noose gripping my neck.

I should recap, because honestly, I am a bit confused myself.

I had been caught stealing one too many potions of an . . . *illicit* nature . . . and the authorities knew of my charms. So they rightfully organised all the legal proceedings with me out of earshot of anyone but a deaf sheriff.

I wasn't too worried none then though. Like I said, I could talk my way out of any situation, given the chance.

All I had to do was wait.

The fools hadn't thought to gag me for all their plans, and they had to cart me past someone who could hear eventually, right?

That's what aggravated me most as they tightened the noose around my neck, because who had a chance to speak—even though my current company could hear—when being executed next to the Bandit King himself?

The crowds were out in droves, here to watch the fabled outlaw meet his end. They chanted, "The Bandit King is dead! Long live the bandit king!" They were fans of his work, really, but that didn't stop them from coming in the masses to watch him dance the gallows jig.

The poor clerk was reading out the list of executees and their crimes, necessary official proceedings lost to the din of the crowds. They got to my name and read out my charge without much thought. As the executioner placed the hood over my head, she asked for any last words—as was my right—but they, too, were lost in the din.

So much for talking my way out of that one. Who would have thought my greatest weakness was a cheering crowd?

The Bandit King came next, and the crowds quieted to listen to his final musings. I didn't really care for it. I would have said something much more useful.

The drums started, and I sighed, grating my neck against the coarse bite of the rope. Soon, I could leave this embarrassment behind me.

The dreadful beat reached its morbid crescendo, but instead of the click of the floor falling out from under me, there was a gunshot, and then a scream that rippled throughout the crowds. Then there was a fight all around me. The executioner cried out before someone cut my rope and carted me away.

Now don't get me wrong, I was grateful for this, honest I was. But I still had a noose squeezing my neck as well as a hood over my head. The world was translated to me through the pinpoints of light that made it through the cloth weave, and all I could smell was my own bad breath. I was thrown over a horse like a dead deer and then was the unwilling participant of a daring chase out of town.

It was some hours before I was finally lifted off the horse and plonked down by a fire. Someone removed my hood and swore, "That ain't our Bandit King! We got the wrong lad!"

So here I was, with a gun pointed at my head, the noose still tied around my neck. It was quiet, out in the wilderness by the crackling fire, so I finally had a chance to work my magic.

"Gentlemen," I said with a smile, the stars that spilled out over the deep blue velvet sky trembled as my magic did its thing, "I might just be the Bandit King you need."

"And how's that?" Their apparent leader in the absence of the King stepped forward, pulling the hammer back on his six-shooter for effect. "Our lad is now dead on account of these nitwits, not thinking to check under the hood before the daring escape."

"That's exactly how's that." I chuckled, and concentrated my magic—this one needed a bit of work and I was tired. I had to ignore the bitter taste of chalky silver in my mouth. "Your band has a reputation for its smarts. I'm guessing that was the King's doing. Well, how would it look if word got out that the band rescued the wrong man? You would be the laughingstock of the criminal world. Best avoid that, methinks."

"How can we avoid it?"

"By claiming you succeeded, and letting me take on the role."

"But he's dead. The Bandit King is dead."

"Yes, yes," I stood, and the bandits stepped back uneasily. "But no one else knows that. You killed the executioner, I heard, the only one close enough in the confusion to know who was who. I can be your new leader. The Bandit King is dead . . ." I lifted my hands for them to cut my binds.

They eyed each other, lowering their weapons as the magic silver tongue did its thing.

The acting leader pulled out his knife and cut my binds. "Long live the Bandit King."

Storm in a Teacup

Plathack shivered, his scales bristling against each other as he cradled the source of warmth between his claws.

The storm was fierce. It raged below the observation deck of the suborbital station. Sheets of ice shattered in the torrents and clattered against the planet facing panels, and the howling . . . Plathack had to drown it from his mind with meditative techniques.

He focused on the cup of tea, soaking in the warmth through the scales on his hands. Those humans might be strange, but they knew how to deal with a stormy day, *tea and biscuits*.

"Field team is breaching the upper stratosphere, sir. The shuttle should be docking momentarily." Sarah was on shift operating the control deck.

Plathack always found her to be the more sensible human on this expedition, unlike the ones who volunteered to go on the repair run through this storm. Poor Gythnat let herself get dragged along. She couldn't stand the thought of a botched repair job.

"Thank you for the update, Comm. Tech Sarah. If you don't mind me asking, you seem rather flat today?"

There was a change in her posture, her shoulders drooping, and Plathack sighed in relief, *a successful initiation of small talk. The cross-cultural training had worked out well.*

It did seem strange to him that humans enjoyed small talk in most situations. He found it a difficult concept to grasp professionally, but his hard work in understanding and then commenting on the subtle differences with the crew was starting to pay off.

"Ah . . ." she hesitated. "Sorry, sir. It's just hard spending such a long time away from my children."

"Oh?" *She's apologising. For what?* He clicked against the teacup with his claws. "Yes, it is hard to be away from your offspring for so long."

There was a clamour and a hiss of air. "Field shuttle docked," the platform's AI announced.

"Ah," Plathack beamed, "Our crewmates have returned safely."

The docking bay doors screeched open and three sopping wet crewmates stood in the bay. They were soaked in icy mud. The field team consisted of two humans and the only other Liman on the station other than Plathack.

"Mission success, sir!" Roger beamed.

"Yeah, just a bent antenna. There was really no need for Gythnat to come along at all." Dan reported.

Gythnat slinked down onto her haunches and started scraping the mud from her scales. She shot Plathack a bitter look, and he didn't press her any further.

"Excellent work then, crew. Perhaps you two should clean yourselves up?" Plathack suggested to the humans.

"Aye aye, sir!" Roger saluted.

"Yeah guys," Sarah laughed, "Hit the showers and don't take all the hot water!"

"Yes, ma'am," Dan replied, "Can't guarantee that Roger won't, though . . . Ow!"

"I just can't resist a nice, long, hot shower after an icy day!" Roger took swipes at Dan as they squelched across the observation deck to the human quarters.

Sarah laughed as they went, "Hey!" she cried, "You lot are getting mud everywhere!"

The two humans left the platform, and the doors sealed shut behind them. A *ping* popped up on Sarah's console and she attended to it as Gythnat stood up, having scraped most of the mud from her golden scales.

"I don't get these humans, Plathack. They're all crazy! Those two whooped and cheered as we rattled through that obscene storm and stopped to look at every lashing of lightning while we repaired the antenna!"

"Well, you were safe. You *were* wearing faraday suits, no?" Plathack slurped from his tea with a slithering tongue.

"Of course, but it's still lunacy!" She finished scraping the mud from her legs and flicked it onto the floor. "And now they retreat from the torrents of rain to subject themselves to even more water? It boggles the mind!"

"I know it's odd, Gythnat. But humans usually take comfort from hot water like that." He held up the teacup. "Whether ingesting it or throwing it over their bodies in those showers. I'm sure we act strangely to them as well."

"That's a fair assessment, Plathack . . . I'm going to go curl up under the red lamps."

"Enjoy yourself!" Plathack waved Gythnat off and turned back to Sarah. "Oh . . ." Liquid flowed from her eyes. "Comm. Tech Sara, I believe you are displaying negative emotions by crying."

"Oh, what? Oh yes, sir, I'm so sorry! It's just that my husband sent me a video. I missed my baby's first steps!" The tears intensified, along with a pained gasping noise, "My little baby!"

"Oh my . . ." Plathack thought quickly.

My fellow human is in distress. It seems as if she is asphyxiating . . . I need to help her. He glanced down at his tea . . . *Warm water thrown over the body!*

Plathack rushed over to Sarah and tipped his tea cup over her head. She stifled a gasp and went rigid as the warm liquid dripped down her hair and saturated her clothes. She turned on Plathack, teeth bared, eyes scrunched shut.

Ah, yes, a smile. And she's stopped crying.

Sarah took a deep breath and turned from Plathack, storming from the room.

With a satisfied clicking of claw on teacup, Plathack turned back to the raging storm below.

"Another successful interaction with my human crew."

The Hammer on the Bridge

Garven grimaced, rolling his shoulders, fatigued from the weight of the gravity cuffs which dug into his wrists. He and his captor entered the sleek lift compartment, and the doors hissed shut before them.

The pleasant ding, the computerised voice that welcomed them, and the soothing corporate music were all contrary to the kidnapping that had just taken place.

"Are they too tight?" Blailock was leaning on his techno-lance as the lift lurched into action, but stirred at Garven's discomfort. He tapped away at the display on his wrist and the cuffs whirred with mechanisms as they expanded and the artificial weight lightened. "Better?"

"Yes," Garven rolled his shoulders, he felt some relief in his aching muscles and blood started circulating back through his wrists, "Thank you."

"Sorry for the initial settings." Blailock slid his visor up and he smiled sheepishly. "That was a bit intense back there."

"I'm aware," Garven said cautiously.

The small lift compartment dinged repeatedly as they moved through the floors to the Deathknell's bridge.

The levels flashed on the main readout, along with the names of the departments: *Accounting, Weapons Division, Brig, Torture Chamber, Human Resources, Sales, Engineering, Life Support, Break Room.*

"You," Garven hesitated, "You don't seem that bad."

Blailock shrugged, his sleek black hunter's armour shifted against his muscular form. "It's just a job, really."

"Just a job?" Garven laughed. "You cut through my bots like a surgeon with a scalpel. That's passion, that's . . ."

"Why thank you, Garven." Blailock was beaming, "Your bots weren't pushovers neither. How did you get their AI to coordinate like that?"

"Trial and error," Garven said. "How did you program your techno-lance to phase through their shields?"

"I used to be a maintenance tech on a government hauler, awful working conditions. Every time we were raided, the fine print categorised it as us treating with non-government entities and docked our pay. You had to get crafty to keep in the black. Being a henchman on the Deathknell pays much better, keeps me active, and even if I disagree with corporate, I enjoy the team. Have you met Daybane?"

Garven nodded.

"His wife hosts the best game nights. Never would have met them him unless I signed up with Overlord."

"Um," Garven hesitated again, "I'm pretty sure Starnaught killed Daybane . . ."

"Oh," Blailock took a moment to process that.

"You didn't know?"

"Corporate has us all wear matching uniforms. It's hard to tell us apart on duty."

"Oh, I'm sorry."

"Nah, it's not so bad since we unionised. His wife will get benefits, I suppose." He glanced up at the level display. "We'll be there soon. Are you an asthmatic? Do you have any lung conditions?"

"No?"

"Good. Overlord likes to be a bit dramatic."

The lift hummed to a halt and the doors parted. The bridge was dim, lit by red floor lighting along the main path, which cut through the command consoles on either side. A smoke machine hissed beneath the floor tiling, excessively filling the room with red lit fog, while a tall, robed figure stood at the end. He looked out over the hull of the Deathknell from an observation platform.

"Greetings, Lady Starnaught," Overlord's voice reverberated throughout the bridge speakers as Blailock led Garven towards the observation deck. "Welcome to the Deathknell." Overlord turned, revealing an aging face that had gone through too much Botox, and froze. "Lights." The Bridge's lights came on, brightening the black tiling, "Vents." Somewhere, vents whirred into life, sucking the artificial smoke and fog from the room.

"Blailock," Overlord gestured to Garven. "Who is this?"

"Garven, My Lord. He's Starnaught's best friend."

"Why is Starnaught's best friend on my bridge?"

"I couldn't find Starnaught's wife on the Defender."

"So you brought his . . . friend? No offence, Garven, but why would I want you here?"

"My Lord," Blailock sighed, "You wanted to entice Starnaught into a risky rescue mission. I couldn't find his wife. So I captured his best friend."

"Why would he risk his life for a friend? Don't you know anything, Blailock? Why would a hero like Starnaught do anything that desperate for a friend?"

"My Lord . . ."

"Silence! I don't pay you for initiative. I pay you to follow orders and sow despair across the galaxy."

"My Lord . . ."

"When I want to lead Starnaught into a trap, I need bait."

"My Lord . . ." Blailock was growing irritated.

"And I want good quality bait. Again, Garven, no offence."

Blailock pointed with his lance and all but roared, "My Lord!"

Overlord turned and froze again, "Oh."

A single little freighter was jetting through the void towards the Deathknell's bridge.

"He is hailing us, My Lord," one of the crew members said.

"Bring him up."

A screen flickered into life upon the observation deck. A weary-looking soldier in a bulky EVA battle suit looked back. "Overlord."

"Starnaught."

"Where is my friend?"

Overlord turned to Blailock with two thumbs up, mouthing, *"Okay, good work."* He turned back to the projection of Starnaught. "We have him, right here on our bridge, noble hero. And he drew you marvellously into my net, FIRE!"

The ship vibrated as the two eternity cannons on either side of the Deathknell's hull raised out of their compartments and tracked Starnaught's ship.

"I was hoping to avoid unpleasantness." Starnaught's voice died into static as the screen winked out.

"I'm sure you were," Overlord cackled.

The observation deck flashed with blinding white light and the deck reverberated with the energy that was expelled from the cannons. When visuals returned, there were two trailing streams of tumultuous red energy which had collided with the freighter and obliterated it into an expanding debris cloud.

"Blailock," Overlord turned from the scene, "You get a promotion! As for you," he turned to Garven, "As our business is concluded, we can offer you a company shuttle to the closest . . ."

"Incoming!" another crew member cried.

They all turned back to the remains of the destroyed freighter. One piece of debris was hurtling straight for them.

"Our shields will deflect it." Overlord said.

"No," the first one paled, "It's rocket propelled, it's, it's Starnaught!"

"Magnify," Blailock ordered.

Starnaught's image was magnified on the observation deck screen. Sure enough, he was tearing through the vacuum in his bulky EVA battle suit, making a beeline for the hull with a power hammer in his hands.

"Well," Overlord said, admiration creeping into his voice, "Shoot him?"

The eternity cannons sent vibrations throughout the hull as they tracked the tiny figure, but they were too bulky and slow to lock onto him. Anti-fighter guns emerged next and fired at the figure, but he was too small, dancing around projectiles designed for crafts one thousand times his size. His boosters fired to slow his descent as he made the hull and his boots mag sealed him in place.

"Well, shoot him!" Overlord cried.

"My Lord, we don't have small enough arms to target a single person on the hull." A crewmember explained.

"Send out void warriors."

"The closest dock is the maintenance hatch. It'll take ten minutes to send out anyone with anything more than a blowtorch, and he is advancing on the observation deck too quickly."

Overlord and his minions watched in stunned silence as Starnaught charged up the length of the Deathknell towards them.

"Do you mean to say that we have no antipersonnel defences? Nothing at all?" Overlord said.

"My Lord," a crewmember stepped forward reading from a data pad, "We mentioned the risk in our requisition meeting last month and you said we didn't have the budget allocation for something that wouldn't happen."

"Well, it's happening now!" Overlord gestured angrily at the charging Starnaught.

"Yes, My Lord. That's why we resent you *offing* the foreman when argued with you about it."

"How about I *off* you?"

"You can't My Lord. In the new Employee Agreement, you cannot *off* a minion for a decision that you yourself made. You'll have to pay out my family half the company's worth . . . You should have installed the anti-personnel cannons."

"We didn't have the budget!"

"You spent half a million credits redirecting the heat exhaust from our reactors to make the Deathknell's logo pulsate!"

"Rebranding was an important part of our business model!" Overlord blustered.

"You know what else is a part of our business model? Killing our arch nemesis when he's . . . he's here."

The whole bridge turned back to the observation screen, where Starnaught peered in from the other side. He sighted Garven and nodded, then powered on his hammer, which pulsed with green energy, and started swinging.

"He's . . . he's not going to be able to break through that, is he? We do have sub space shielding?" Overlord asked.

"Not on the first twenty swings," the crewmember with the data pad said.

The dull silence of the hammer repeatedly hitting the screen filled the room.

Blailock slowly clicked his visor back in place and helped Garven do the same. He tapped on his wrist computer, his boots and all the minions' boots sealed magnetically in place. He then helped Garven with his mag boots, too.

On the nineteenth swing, the glass shattered, the atmosphere rushed out into the void, carrying a screaming Overlord with it.

Starnaught marched through the broken screen and scanned the many enemies arrayed against him. Then he started gesturing. It looked like he was talking.

Blailock tapped on his wrist computer again and Starnaught's voice came through everyone's personal comms.

"Can you read me?"

"Yes," Blailock answered.

"I am just here for my friend. Are we going to fight?"

"No."

Starnaught hesitated. His hammer drooped. "Why not?"

"Well, our payroll is wired through his neural link," Blailock gestured with his techno-lance to the flailing Overlord as he tumbled through space. "I am off the clock permanently now. No reason to fight."

"Oh," Starnaught gazed around the bridge, "Anyone else?"

"Well," another crewmember spoke up, "Now that the league will dissolve, I could use the severance pay to start my micro brewery."

There was a murmuring of agreement throughout the bridge crew minions.

"Yeah, most of us have side hustles which have been doing well. It's only smart in this economy to cover your bases if you have a flexible job. We should be fine." A minion said.

"Well, *I* want to fight!" A console tech stood up. "But I'm not signed off for combat and HR will dock my next pay if I do that."

"Yeah," Blailock nodded, "HR are salaried until the dissolution of the league entirely, better not risk it. Speaking of, someone contact Mindy and let her know what's happened."

"So," Garven said, "We can go?"

"Yeah, sure," Blailock removed his binds.

Garven ambled over to Starnaught, who took him under one bulky arm.

"Hey," Blailock called before they left through the broken screen. They turned. "Once this is all cleared up, let's get a drink. I can spec out your bot shields and you can teach me some of the AI programming."

"Yeah, that would be nice," Garven said. "Ah . . . see ya, I guess."

Blailock waved them off as Starnaught and Garven stepped out onto the hull and jettisoned away to safety.

APOTHECARY

Mungun surged through the undergrowth and dove away from the maws of the alpha wolf. Its teeth snapped shut around nothing but thistle, and Mungun spun to clobber it savagely in the face with his lit torch.

The wolf whelped and stumbled away in an explosion of embers as Mungun righted himself. He bellowed at the dozens of glinting eyes in the depths of the night, reflecting the blazing fire which he held aloft.

"COME ON!" He screamed, "MUNGUN HAS ENOUGH FIRE FOR ALL YOUR JAWS!"

The alpha recovered in the brush and released and low, pained howl. The glinting eyes faded into the woods as the wolves retreated. The alpha shot one last snarl at Mungun before hobbling off.

Mungun bellowed a victorious roar, beating his chest before getting woozy and stumbling.

"Not yet," he gasped, "Not yet."

He gripped his wounded arm—not from the wolves. It had a rash that burned more with each passing day. It propelled him on this quest to find the apothecary on the mountain top.

After a cold, restless night, Mungun continued his journey up the slopes. He battled bears, dragons and foul, slinking lizards.

A week of toil passed. He reached the top of the mountain where the air was thin and suffered the chest to breathe, and he found the apothecary's hut nestled within a grove of pine trees. The hut was simple at a glance, constructed from mud and logs, seeming hardy enough.

The grove grew along a rocky ridge that overlooked the mountain range.

It was beautiful, but Mungun had no time for that.

He limped through the leather flap at the entrance and found a young man in heavy furs sitting behind a large, flat boulder with clay tablets stacked upon it. The rest of the hut behind him was hidden by a partition made from thin slats of wood.

"Good morning sir, do you have an appointment?" The young man asked.

"No," Mungun panted. "I need to see the apothecary, though."

"Have a seat," the young man pointed to some furs along the wall, where an assortment of different patients suffering from varying ailments and injuries were waiting. "It might be a bit of a wait."

"Thank you." Mungun nodded politely at the other patients and slumped down onto one of the furs.

After several hours of watching the other patients circulate, he was finally called around to see the apothecary. He went behind the partition and found an old woman in worn furs working at a flat boulder with a mortar and pestle. He was assailed by the pungent scent of gathered herbs and potions in clay pots which lined the walls on stone shelves. There was a low cot along the far wall.

"Hello," she said without looking up from grinding away at her mortar and pestle. "How can I help you today?"

Mungun sat awkwardly on the cot as the apothecary turned to look at him. "Um, I got his rash last week, and decided I needed to see someone about it. I spent that time journeying up the mountain and battling beasts just to get to you."

"Hmmm." The apothecary took Mungun's arm and inspected the rash. "It's probably just an infection. Go home and get plenty of water and rest, and if it hasn't gone down in two weeks, you should come back because it's probably something worse." The apothecary patted Mungun's arm and smiled, before gesturing to the exit.

Mungun trudged out into the cold mountain air, taking in the vista of snow-laden mountain forests laid out before him. "Well, that was a waste of time."

BROTHERS IN HARM

've never had a counter assassination mission before. I might even know the target . . . I might even get on with them.

Personal feelings aside, this was going to be tricky due to the "industrial knowledge" of the "client". Translation—the blighter knows what I'll do and how I'll do it.

The target's target—some noble—was travelling to some big parley in neutral territory. That would take his party through Crackling Wood, a dense wilderness of half-dead trees, rotting foliage, and a-lot-a moss.

There was one good point to jump a mark there, right as the road rounds a blind corner. So I picked a spot that overlooked that point. The tricky part here was arriving *before* my colleague.

I arrived *two stinking days* before.

It was a breezy morning that rattled the half dead woods in the pale light. My cloak rustled as I pulled it tight; covered with stuck on branches so I could blend into the cursed brush.

I picked a nice spot, nestled next to a mossy log.

And I waited.

For two days I lay still.

My muscled cramped, my trousers damped . . . you know why. Yet my target never arrived and my vexations grew. Despite my angst, I couldn't move. I'd reveal my position the instant my mark arrived, knowing my luck.

Two days of nothing is a long time for doubt and panic to set in.

But I stuck to discipline, and waited, and then waited more.

Insanity supplanted boredom. My stomach ached and my head throbbed and in the pale light of a new morning I wanted to give in; until I was roused by the clip-clop of hooves upon the road.

I dared not even breathe, aiming my crossbow at the thicket by the ambush point, in case I missed my mark slipping through in the dead of night.

The noble's vanguard rounded the bend, then his entourage, then he himself, bored and proper in rich clothed splendour.

But no target, no ambush . . . I would have to spirit away and scour the road for threats.

Then a click, a whistle, and a whoosh of air.

A crossbow bolt flew and pierced the noble's heart.

A bolt from the log I was nestled by.

Despite my discipline, I jolted. I sprung from the brush and training my bow on the log. It was not a log at all; it was my mark, my fellow assassin, wearing a cloak with much better camouflage than mine.

"Arranflor, you ass!" I cried.

The log sniggered, "You might want to run, friend. That noble's guard think you're the killer."

I turned to the road.

The guards sighted me, foolishly revealed, holding crossbow in hand. They were shouting, drawing swords, dismounting, and wading into the dry brush.

"Beers at the tavern?" Arranflor hissed.

"You're buying, prick." I bolted as the guards pursued, running past the inconspicuous log.

APEX

The herd moved across the savannah into the inviting green and a new danger lay ready in wait. The sun was high and bore down on the grazers as they foraged for food and moisture. They had stopped short of the long grass, which was tall and dry, and had followed the pasture to the edge of a gorge.

Tensions were high, hemmed up against cover for predators and a death trap of razor sharp rock. But they had to eat. All that was behind them was the shrivelling savannah and a thicket of trees wavering on the horizon.

Broadhoof ignored all of this as he nuzzled his way through the tuft of grass. There was a cluster of rocks nestled within it and they tasted damp. He tongued the moisture and lapped up the critters with a crunch. Not as satisfying as the tuft of grass itself, but the moisture was a relief under the unbearable sun.

The herd made their way towards these plains for some days. Gnarlhorn suggested that there would be more green here, as other herds had fled it early, warning of a new pack of predators moving into the area.

"Less grazers more grass," he had bleated.

But Broadhoof was skittish. More grass meant more places for those predators to hide.

Gnarlhorn said their herd was faster than the others, and trotted on despite the danger.

Broadhoof did not protest much. After all, Gnarlhorn was herd leader at the time. He wasn't herd leader anymore though.

No, there wasn't any nonsense about alphas struggling to remove him. All that had happened was that Longtail wandered off in another direction yesterday and the herd all followed him.

Gnarlhorn nudged Broadhoof off the tuft he was munching on, and he trotted off with a grunt to the pasture closer to the long grass. He perked up as he noticed more of the herd moving, and realised they were now following *him*.

I guess I'm herd leader now.

He settled down to graze. The long grass was rustling and Twitchear suddenly jolted. The rest of the herd stopped grazing and scanned the area, listening and smelling.

Twitchear had the best ears in the herd. She once bolted a split second before the sabre cat got poor Strongknee.

So if she jolted, the herd would pay attention.

They craned their necks.

Waiting

Broadhoof smelled nothing.

After a moment, they all returned to their grazing.

Then there was a whistle of several strange sounding birds, a grunt, and then a sharp stick flew from the grass and grazed Broadhoof's leg.

Strange creatures erupted from the grass in a line.

They ran on two legs with most of their fur on their heads and coordinated, like lions, but nothing like lions. They yelled and chanted and the herd scattered, stampeding around the gorge.

Broadhoof was at the rear, but not for long. The small cut on his leg was painful, but nothing to worry about.

Then there was a crack and one of the boulders on the edge of the gorge was toppled by other predators and the herd had to leap over it.

With the pain in his leg, Broadhoof barely made it. He clipped his hooves mid-leap and tumbled over. Two of the predators rushed in with strange claws fashioned from wood and stone, jabbing at him. He bucked up and brayed, menacing them with his horns until they backed off.

Then they scattered, making a gap for the savannah.

Broadhoof took his opportunity and shot out of there like the time the sabre cat got Strongknee, leaving the predators in his wake. They trotted after him, but on their stumpy two legs, they fell behind quickly.

After a time, the heat was building up in Broadhoof faster than he could cool down, and the pain in his leg was growing.

He trotted to a stop to find himself alone. The rest of the herd was moving further away into the green on the other side of the gorge.

The desolation of the shrinking savannah engulfed him. No matter, he would wait for these predators to retreat, and then would rejoin the herd . . . but as he gazed back towards the gorge, they were still running towards him, wavering on the distant heat currents.

Broadhoof snorted derisively. They would never catch him.

But their steady progress had him on edge. He started ambling towards the outcropping of trees on the horizon. There would be water there, and cover from those things. Not that he was worried about them. Nothing could sustain that pace for longer than a few minutes.

As Broadhoof journeyed, his wound grew more burdensome, but he put his mind off it, trying to figure out how they could not smell the predators before they attacked. They were probably smeared in mud and other scents of the land. That was the only explanation.

It had been some hours now.

Broadhoof was suffering from heat and pain and exhaustion. He looked over his shoulder to see that the predators had been steadily gaining on him. In renewed panic, he high tailed the remainder of the distance to the trees.

He collapsed once he reached the thicket. The shade was cool, and the predators were now far, far behind. He closed his eyes and rested. He could find water when he woke. It was bubbling somewhere close by, it was not far. But for now, rest.

The smell woke him.

Whatever those things had smeared on their bodies, it had worn off somehow. Broadhoof shifted up with aching limbs and a dry mouth. He was still overheating, even though the afternoon sun was low.

He needed water.

But he stood and peered out over the savannah, catching a terrifying glimpse of the pack of predators closing in. The mud and scent masks ran off their bodies as they glistened.

Where were they getting that water from?

How could they still be running?

Some held the young in their arms and kept up, even the old kept up with the group. And then there were the others, the ones out in front. They had those strange claws and horns in their hands.

Broadhoof needed a new plan. Exhaustion be dammed. He had tried going in a straight line. Maybe if he zigzagged through the thicket of trees, they wouldn't be able to tell which direction he went.

He upped and bolted deeper into the thicket. Every collision of hoof with dirt sent shock waves of pain through his leg. It also throbbed through his head and muscles as they cried out with dehydration. By the time he stopped his mad dash through the trees, the afternoon was deepening and he was on the brink of collapse.

The edge of the thicket was nearby. He crawled towards the edge and lay down, dead to the world.

Broadhoof was awoken again by heat and pain. The sun was peering through the tree canopy, and the cicadas were singing a deafening chorus. He bit back a groan as he made himself stand.

The water bubbled nearby. He could taste it on his tongue. He decided to follow the scent, but froze when he scented something else, the predators.

They were close.

But how?

He had run a maze through these trees. They couldn't have picked the direction he travelled . . . unless . . . Broadhoof peered down at the deep gouges he had made in the earth with his passing.

My tracks?

What were these things?

A twig snapped, a bird whistled, Broadhoof's heart spiked, and he bolted from the trees again.

He broke the clearing and made it two whole gallops before his leg gave up on him and his body refused the continued, constant effort. He collapsed, braying and crying in pain.

As he thrashed, the predators emerged from the trees. They moved slowly now knowing he was spent. The old ones sat by on the tree roots and rocks and took the young in their arms as the mature-looking ones approached cautiously.

It looked like they were settling down to graze.

But graze what? There was nothing to eat here . . . oh. Broadhoof sagged his head onto the ground, defeated.

They grunted things to each other.

"Put it out of its misery quickly, do it cleanly." The pack leader said to a younger one.

The sounds had no meaning to Broadhoof as the younger one stepped forward with a claw of wood and stone in its hand.

"We appreciate your death, great beast." It said, caressing Broadhoof's neck.

He was terrified, but something about the creature's voice, something about its touch, was soothing.

"We will honour your body. Nothing shall be wasted as it sustains the tribe."

He raised his strange claw to strike, and Broadhoof closed his eyes.

THE UNLUCKIEST MAN IN THE WORLD

General Roan shivered as he left the heated compartment of the government car. It wasn't just cold, but apocalyptic considering the usually humid area, blasted by the chilly winds under the dark skies which pulsed with a myriad of colours. A canvas tent waited before him within the hastily erected camp, its flap billowing in the wind while the two heavily armed guards on either side stood motionless.

Roan grimaced, probably the two best soldiers in the region to be trusted with this detail, and they suffered for it out here. Pulling his cloak tight around his rickety frame, he pushed through the winds and the guards saluted.

"Good evening General. High Commander Lee is waiting for you."

Roan returned something that barely resembled a salute, ignoring the way the guards made cursory eye contact with each other. He didn't become a general because of his exploits following protocol.

"Is General Nemis here?" Roan asked.

"Sir," the guard pointed to a second car pulling up behind Roan's.

A tall, wiry man in his early sixties was let out by his driver and he marched down the path towards them without openly reacting to the cold winds.

"Good evening, General," the guards saluted.

He saluted back, "Men, General."

"General . . ." Roan replied stiffly. "Shall we get out of this cold?" He eyed the guards. "Sorry."

The guards made cursory eye contact again, but Nemis was already pushing past them to enter the tent. Roan sighed and made to follow when the sky pulsed with pink lights. He hesitated and followed the direction of the pulse. The point of origin ended on the horizon, past a bleak expanse that dominated the landscape after the edge of the forward operating base. A fluctuating ball of light raged against the dark skies.

Roan sighed again.

"They are waiting for you, General," the guard was holding the tent flap.

"Good man." Roan nodded and entered the chaotic command tent.

High Commander Lee was bent over a topographical map, ignoring Nemis as he announced himself. Aids and analysts operated the communications and survey equipment in an urgent manner. Some weathered scientist was over Lee's shoulder. She was proclaiming doomsday predictions and the like.

"Lee," Roan said easily.

Lee looked up, and a wave of relief washed over his strained features. "Roan, thank God for you. This is Doctor Tyson. She can give you and Nemis a brief rundown on the current situation."

Tyson rolled her eyes and homed in on the two generals. "Gentlemen, what we have here is a . . ."

"Catastrophic strobe shift failure." Roan said, perusing the map. "Your experiments altering light speed to communicate instantly with our facilities on Mars shifted one too many dimensions. Now some radioactive element from one of them is threatening to spread out over the Earth if uncontained . . . am I reading that right?"

"Yes . . ." Tyson hesitated. "How . . ."

"You did send us briefing packets. We aren't grunts, Doctor. Not to worry, I have implemented a solution already."

"You what?" Nemis spun on him. "You gave orders without High Command's approval?"

"Good to know you're a general with initiative, Nemis." Roan sighed. "Lee wouldn't have brought us onboard if he already had a plan. I saved time before more of our dimension was compromised."

"And what is your plan?" Lee asked.

"Yeah," Tyson fretted, "Nothing we have implemented works. The area around the device is so radioactive that it's frying our robots' circuits. And due to the blending of dimensions, Murphy's Law seems to have been exponentially applied to our reality. So every conscious entity meets untold calamity before they can get close. A precision strike would just make things worse . . ."

"I sent in Corporal Fortis." Roan said.

The entire command tent went silent.

"Corporal James Fortis?" Lee asked.

"Yes," Roan said.

"Corporal James 'Rotter' Fortis?" Nemis yelled.

"Yes," Roan repeated.

"Rotter?" Tyson asked.

Lee sighed, "It's an acronym. R.O.T.R. *Rest Of The Rabbit.* Corporal Fortis is one of the unluckiest soldiers in any army anywhere."

"Yeah, he was once voted most likely to die from a frozen jet stream falling on his head in the middle of the desert." Nemis interjected.

"From an anvil falling from that plane's cargo, actually," Roan corrected.

"And you're sending him in to save the world?" Nemis sneered.

"Yes," Roan rubbed his temple, "You see, he is most prepared to face the bad luck plaguing the area from the Murphy's Law shift."

"I sure hope you're right," Lee said, "because if he fails, the world will become a radioactive wasteland."

* * *

Corporal James 'Rotter' Fortis cursed when the canvassed transport truck hit a pothole and veered off-road onto the unforgiving terrain of the heath. Something burst, a tyre probably, and the rear wheels were sinking into a bog. He revved the engine and saw the shower of mud flit out as he watched through the side mirror.

He smashed the steering wheel with another curse and the air bag deployed, knocking him back into the chair with a grunt.

"Damn this," He muttered.

He pushed the deflating air bag aside and hopped out the door, sinking knee deep into the bogged ground and muttering to himself as he squelched to the back of the canvassed truck. Luckily, he wore extra sturdy gum boots over his hazmat overalls, wouldn't want to snag it on any debris in the bog. If he noticed the strobing chromatic colours across the dark skies up ahead, he paid no attention to them.

"Rotter?" A voice crackled through his earpiece. "Rotter, report." It was General Roan.

"Yeah General, I'm okay," he lamented as he let down the back of the truck and climbed into the dark compartment. "Truck is cooked, about a twenty-minute walk from the point of origin."

"Twenty minutes?" Another voice cut in, "If we wait that long, we'll reach the point of no return and we'll all be done for!"

"Who was that?" James replied as he sat over the all terrain quad bike he had loaded up into the back of the canvassed truck.

"That was General Nemis." Roan said.

"Is he going to be complaining constantly?" James asked.

"Probably."

"Well, it's a good thing communications fail the closer we get to the point of origin." He keyed the ignition and the quad bike roared to life.

Roan laughed back over the earpiece, "Can you salvage the truck?"

"No sir, it's cooked," James accelerated and launched the quad bike from the back of the truck. It cleared the bog to jolt back onto the road. "I'm carrying on with the backup vehicle."

"Who on Earth would load a back-up vehicle?" Nemis asked.

"Someone who expects misfortune," Roan answered for him. "Good luck, Rotter."

"Thank you, sir," James said before the communications fizzled out.

The wind was cold and buffeted him on the quad bike as he tore down the road towards the ominous, pulsating glow. It was a good thing he wore extra thermal layers under his hazmat suit. Sure, it was a bit warm in the truck, but he expected it to fail. The gusts of wind blew out from the glowing point of origin and a thundering bolt of lightning tore overhead. Then sheets of rain fell suddenly, and he found himself squinting through the downpour.

His quad bike kicked up a stone from the road, and it bounced into the floodlights. They shattered and went dark.

James reached into his pack for the super strength hand held flood light and attached it to his helmet. The beam was narrow but potent, enough to see the road through the deluge.

A few minutes later, he drove through the open chain link gates into the research compound and his Geiger counter started rattling like crazy. The main laboratory was just ahead, a grey box set into the middle of the facility. Pulses of amber light shot through the windows and the crumbling roof to shine into the sky. As he drew closer, the amber light shifted to yellow, then violet, green, and back to amber. The rain cleared and James slipped in a puddle as he alighted from his quad bike and smashed into the ground.

He took the impact on his wrists, which would have shattered if he had not worn adequate wrist guards.

With a grunt, he got up and shuffled carefully into the main lab.

As he passed through the shattered glass doors, a snag caught his hazmat suit and tore it open. Warnings blared within his suit that a breach had been detected and deadly levels of radiation were leaking in. He swore again and calmly pulled out his duct tape to seal up the breach, confident that the second hazmat suit he was wearing underneath had not been breached or he would already be dead.

He made his way through the lobby and up the stairwell to the top floor. The stairs were strewn with detritus and his wet clumsy gum boots caused him to slip and shuffle. So he removed them, confident that his combat boots—enwrapped in his hazmat suit—would give him more purchase. He managed to avoid the debris with minimal slips and falls.

The higher he climbed and the closer he got to the device, the more the heat intensified. Sweat pooled within the doubled up hazmat suits at the pits, waist and at his feet.

His visor fogged, and he cursed. Strapped to the right of his helmet, within his mask, was a little squeeze pump bottle. He gripped it with his teeth and squeezed. The anti-fog spray hit the visor, and the condensation ran off, allowing him to see.

He reached the main research room and as he ducked under the crumbling door frame, a florescent light decided then and there to fall and strike him in the top of the head.

It shattered against his head, but the military helmet he had donned beneath his hazmat suit prevented a concussion. He swore and stumbled, gripping onto the military robot that had died halfway between the door and the device. It was an inert, four-legged creature. Its lifeless camera lens peered back at him.

"You did a great job!" James spat.

He shuffled away from the robot and over to the device, which hummed, rattled, and pulsed with menace under the hole it had torn in the ceiling. He gripped the shut-off valve and with a grunt; he turned it until the device whirred to a halt and the strobing lights stopped.

His Geiger counter stopped crackling as the multi dimensional radiation was cut off, and he breathed a sigh of relief as his comms chirped back to life.

"Rotter, Rotter, do you read?"

"Yes, General, mission accomplished."

"Good work soldier, you've got a hero's welcome waiting for you back here. You just saved the world."

"Lucky me," James laughed, "Returning to base."

He turned from the inert device. The robot was rebooting and started shuffling forwards, obeying its last command. As it ambled across the room like an awkward dog, the floor trembled and cracked; the integrity failing with the extra weight.

"Ah, damn." The floor collapsed out from both of them and he tumbled through to land in a mess of tangled limbs and debris. "Oh, well." He said to himself in a heap, "It's not the end of the world, is it?"

THE PRICE OF WITCHCRAFT

Jaral was shaking, and his voice quavered uncontrollably.

He tried to cover it up with a cough, clearing his throat as if affected by the putrid fumes that hissed from the bubbling cauldron.

He *was* affected by the putrid fumes, mind you. We all were—well, not the witch who cackled at our discomfort—but we all knew it was fear that caused his reaction. Not that I could judge. I was sweating through my tunic. The deep red fabric grew darker with oozing perspiration by the minute.

The decrepit old woman threw a foul herb into the concoction and stirred it in with an oversized ladle, pushing up onto her toes and heaving with her shoulders to move the sludge around. She was exactly as we expected, exactly what we needed to complete our goal, and the only reason we travelled out to this backwater commune in the forest.

"Well?" Jaral managed to squeak. "Will you make the spell for us?"

"Oh, heh, hargh, haragh!" The witch cackled so violently that she fell into a horrid coughing fit, which shuddered throughout her creaking body. "Oh, I can give you what you seek."

"But?" I stepped further into the cramped, hide strewn shelter.

"Well," she heaved as she continued her slow, laborious stirring, "It will cost you both greatly. A deep, *red*, price." She glanced between Jaral and I, a sly, evil gaze that halted on me and stared deep, *deep*, into my heart. "Are you willing to pay the price?" she laughed again, different this time, a low, foreboding murmur.

Jaral sighed and clutched at his purse, then glanced at me. *He was so naïve.*

I steeled myself and gave him a nod, making a show of reaching for my purse as well.

As he turned back to the witch, I drew my dagger and shut my eyes as I slew him.

"What are you doing?" The witch shrieked and jumped back, pulling out her steaming ladle and holding it before her with a splash of boiling fluid.

I shook my head, incredulous, as I wiped the blood from my dagger on my trousers. "I'm paying the red price. Now give me the spell."

"The red price is rubies, you absolute lunatic! I meant it would cost you all of your rubies! What kind of person backstabs their companion for a good luck spell?"

"I . . ." I suddenly felt a hot weight in my gut, ". . . you didn't need a blood sacrifice?"

"Get out of my hovel! Guards! GUARDS!" The witch was shrieking, and a responding commotion sounded from the derelict commune outside.

"Oh," I turned and ran from the hovel, without my spell and without my friend.

ROGUE UNDERDOG UNION

Blades of light lanced towards the Venciliator's observation deck as it streaked through void-space at unfathomable speeds. It was quiet in the richly adorned space, and Brawsh filled the silence with the imagined sounds of a dying home world as yet another disgusting species was subjugated by the Empire.

The doors hissed open and Brawsh clicked his fangs as his aide hurried from clanking metal hallways to the soft carpeted interior of the observation deck.

"Your Excellency," she bowed.

"Reatie," one of his globular eyes darted to acknowledge her and then snapped back to the kaleidoscopic void-space corridor, "From this interruption, I take it we will be arriving presently?"

"Yes, your Excellency. I am patching the Captain of the Venciliator through to you now."

Brawsh winced as the harsh sound of static invaded his space. "Captain?" he asked.

"Ambassador Brawsh, we have received word from Admiral Trithe through the void-comms. She has made contact with the human world and has begun her subjugation."

Brawsh's lips curled back from his red fangs in a cruel smile. "Excellent, we won't have long to wait upon arrival before we hear the lamentations of our new servants. Exerting power, Reatie, that's why I took this position. It's what our kind do."

"Yes, your Excellency," Reatie said.

The Captain announced their arrival over the speakers, "Exiting void-space in three, two, one."

The lances of celestial light lassoed the image of a small blue dot as the ship slowed back into real-space with a dull roar. Their planetary array was in shambles, their satellite orbits littered with the debris of their ruined fleets and installations, empyreal fire from Imperial battle ships had shredded their . . .

Brawsh furrowed his brow. *Where was the Imperial fleet?*

"Captain . . . ?"

"We noticed, scanning for Admiral Trithe now," the Captain said.

Reatie leaned in past Brawsh and scrunched her eyes to see through the prolific wreckage before them. "Where are they?" She asked.

"I have no idea," Brawsh wondered, "They were clearly here. The humans have been all but obliterated."

"Umm," Reatie pointed at a piece of wreckage that drifted in a slow tumble past the observation deck, "Is that?"

The wreckage turned to reveal lettering signifying an Imperial ship . . . '*Acrimony*'.

"That's the Admiral's ship!" Reatie cried. "This wreckage is the Imperial fleet!"

"That can't . . ." Brawsh stuttered as a cold twinge of dread rippled across his hide. "That can't be."

"Ambassador," the Captain's voice broke through his spiralling panic, "We are being hailed by a human vessel."

"What's its location?" Reatie asked.

"Unknown. We aren't detecting the technology required to obliterate our fleet, just a radio signal."

"Home in on that signal!" Brawsh ordered.

The observation screen pulsed as the overlays translated the radio signal into a visual beacon, then zoomed in on a tiny little vessel darting—leisurely—around the wreckage of the Acrimony towards the Venciliator.

"What armaments does that vessel possess?" Brawsh asked.

"Whatever weapons it has equipped must be cloaked. All we detect is rudimentary propulsion, life support, computational power, and the radio signal. Really, we only detected it because they hailed us, Ambassador." The Captain said.

Brawsh set his quivering lips and rallied an air of authority to go with his next words. "Patch them through."

"Greetings, invasion fleet, this is Barry Young. Do you read?"

"We read you, Earthling. This is His Excellency Ambassador Brawsh, are you an ambassador ship?"

"No sir-ee, I'm the guy that vanquished your fleet."

Reatie gasped and looked at Brawsh, who ignored her. "In that ship?"

The overlay zoomed in on Barry's ship as it exited the debris field and came more into view. It was a bulbous mining tug vessel, by the looks of it.

"With ones like it, yeah."

"How? You aren't military?"

"Nah, when your invasion fleet arrived, the military pressed the mining guild into overtime to sustain the defence effort. Overtime pay was not provided . . . the union sent me to make sure the workers weren't taken advantage of."

"You're a . . . Miner?"

"A Mining Union Rep, to be exact, negotiations with the military and CEOs weren't going too well, so we decided to act. Got in past your defences with these lower tech vessels, which were designed to tow mineral rich asteroids. We clogged up your fusion drive exhausts until they exploded."

"You destroyed the invasion fleet with mining tugs?"

"Yeah, anyway. Military said seeing as we were in the area we could be the ones to demand your surrender. You are an ambassador ship, yeah?"

"Yeah . . . but . . . I won't treat with low-class scum! Captain, take us away. We will come back with another fleet."

"Your Excellency," The Captain acknowledged, and the Venciliator pulled away from Barry's mining vessel.

"Well, can't say we didn't try," Barry laughed. "Pull away boys and girls, before she blows."

"What?" Brawsh watched through the observation screen in horror as dozens of other mining tugs came into view, pulling away from the Venciliator and its fusion drive exhaust ports. "Captain?!"

"THERMAL PORTS OVERHEATING, ABANDON SHIP!"

Reatie screamed and bolted from the observation deck as the warning lights and sirens went into overdrive. Brawsh watched the retreating mining vessels, undetectable until now because the Venciliator simply wasn't looking for such low-tech ships.

Just before the nuclear fire engulfed him, Brawsh uttered his final curse, "You troglodyte peasants!"

MIRROR KNIGHT

Tobyn dashed into the atrium of the ruins. The yellowed stone was caked in lichen and creeping green vines. The walls rose up on all sides, cracked and marred by time and ending in an opening skylight that let the cloud filtered sun drift into the dim space.

Water spouted from crumbling fixtures and poured into the fathomless channels that lined the wide space . . . The water was mixed with fresh viscera, that flowed over layers of dried blood from past adventurers.

"No," Tobyn breathed. The towering defender of the ruined temple stood over the freshest corpse, a man who had cut his own throat. "You killed him!" Tobyn roared.

"I showed him the truth of things!" The defender's voice echoed within his ashen helm and reverberated through the ancient stone. "I did not command him to enter this domain. I did not force him to view his own life through the lens of my shield! I am but a sentinel placed here to defend the treasures of this temple from those who are not pure, from those who cannot bear to look into their own shadow and keep their sanity intact! Come now, little squireling, you have entered my domain. Deem to look into your own soul and we shall see if you are worthy!"

Tobyn covered his eyes as the knight hefted his mighty shield of silver glass and turned it in his direction.

"You shy away from your true nature, little one? Leave, or I shall have you leave this world, screaming!" The knight launched forward, each step a trembling rattle.

Tobyn felt his foot slip back as every instinct told him to run from the approaching behemoth. He gripped his feeble dagger in one hand. Tobyn knew what happened to his master. He could not keep his eyes averted from the mirror shield. He gazed into the abyss of his own soul and he lost his mind at the lack he saw there.

Then he took his own life.

Tobyn would not look, but he would not let the Mirror Knight kill him conventionally either. He had to be cleverer than his master.

As the thundering steps of the Mirror Knight drew closer, the flash of an idea sped across Tobyn's mind. He ducked and rolled to the side, discarding his dagger and pulling out his flint and stone, grabbing a torch from a traveller long dead.

With a deft motion, Tobyn lit the flame, and the torch sprung to life. He dashed around the atrium, lighting the long, inert torch sconces upon the walls.

The pale filtered light from the skylight was replaced by an encompassing orange glow.

"You think the light will save you? The light cannot dispel the darkness that lurks within!"

Tobyn ignored the taunting, turning now to face the Knight with his eyes down. He scooped up a poleaxe from another dead hero at his feet and used the shadows of the Mirror Knight—cast from the dancing torch light—to locate his foe.

He could see him now, now he could fight.

The shadow of the knight shifted as he lurched forward, and Tobyn ducked and rolled to the side again, shifting around the mirror shield. He came to his feet, whirling the poleaxe in a wide arc, and struck the knight in the joint of the elbow. The shield clattered from his hands with a pained cry.

The mirror shield skittered across the flooring, dipping into the endless channels that lined the atrium to be carried away, out of reach from them both.

Tobyn risked looking at his foe now. The knight rounded on him, unarmed but covered in ashen plate armour. With a roar, Tobyn struck, slamming the weight of the poleaxe into the knight again and again, battering the ashen coating which drifted away in the still air.

The knight made no move to stop him, made no taunt. He simply stood and shifted with each blow, waiting for Tobyn to realise what lay beneath the buildup of dust over the ages.

With a cry, Tobyn realised too late.

His last blow shed a caked layer of dust from the Knight's breastplate. As it crumbled away, Tobyn tried to shield his eyes, but the knight was upon him. He gripped Tobyn in his mighty arms and pressed his face into the pristine reflective plating on the cuirass.

"Look, child, look deep, look into the depths of your soul . . ."

The knight squeezed as Tobyn tried to scrunch his eyes shut. But the pain was too great. He surrendered to his fate.

What he saw, reflected in the breastplate of the Mirror Knight, was . . . was . . .

Tobyn giggled.

The Knight hesitated, relinquishing his grip to look down as well, and he himself let out a jolly gasp, "Heh."

Tobyn's giggle caught on, and the Knight roared with laughter as he stood back, the shaking of his jolly expression causing Tobyn to laugh all the harder.

The breast plate was a curved design. In the reflection, Tobyn's face was distorted, lending his jaw to be comically large and overly strong. His forehead was oblong, raised and stretched and twisted while his eyes were pinched and squinted. As he laughed, his mouth spread wider in the mirror, causing him to smile more, to laugh more, and so on.

"Truly," The Mirror Knight said, sighing as he took another breath, "You have shown courage, and have the spirit of glee and humour. Together, those are the traits of your soul . . . I deem you worthy!" The knight stepped aside, gesturing the way to the temple's inner sanctum. "Go now, master squire, you have a pure soul. Never let it tarnish like my armour has over the ages."

KINDLING

rugar pulled himself over the slope. The cold ground bit at his numb knuckles and he wheezed a sigh as he found his destination.

It was a Witch Doctor's hovel, although it was more a tarpaulin and an assortment of rods that were playing pretend at being a tent.

Drugar thought it a miracle that it stood against the chilling gales, but he also knew more was at play here than met the eye.

It mattered not how decrepit the Witch Doctor or his hovel was. His village would be proud of him none the less, he would bring back the medicine they needed.

With another wheeze, he hauled himself up and trundled over.

"She's occupied."

Drugar hadn't noticed the hunched figure, stooped low over an inert fire pit.

"Gods!" Drugar gasped, "I thought you a stone."

"If only," the figure—a hale man—looked up from a low hood and smiled weakly. A glint of flame danced deep in his eyes.

"Ah, you're one of them, Fire Wizards." Drugar dragged himself over the frost and sat across from the figure.

He glanced at the fire pit. The Fire Wizard was rubbing two sticks together with hands so cold they could not grasp them properly.

"You out of practice there?" Drugar hacked a laugh from his tired lungs. "People of your kind are said to make the gods tremble. Perhaps the stories are exaggerated?"

The figure smiled wanly again, "I have duelled angels, fought back beasts that clawed their way into our realm and left them smote against the space between worlds . . ."

He was not boasting, Drugar realised, "And yet you struggle to start a mere fire, despite all of that?"

The figure looked at him. "Despite all I am capable of, my daughter lies on death's door in there." He looked at the hovel and sighed. "Kings would butcher thousands for my power, and I would trade it all to have some power over her fate."

"Ah," Drugar sighed and leaned over. He carefully took the sticks from the Fire Wizard's hands and started to heat the kindling with friction. Smoke drifted from the pit. "Sometimes all you can do, is all you can do . . . and that is enough. You brought your daughter here, and now you sit out in the cold while others express their own power. And do you know why?"

The Fire Wizard did not answer.

"Because hope, dear Wizard, hope is the fire of the soul. It is hope you must conjure now."

"I don't know how."

The kindling ignited, a spark of flame caught, and the pit erupted into a gentle, crackling blaze.

"Perhaps she can show you how."

The Fire Wizard followed Drugar's gaze. The Witch Doctor stood at the flap of the hovel and beckoned him over.

With trepidation, he ambled through into the dark interior. Drugar watched with bated breath, and smiled when the dimness was lit by a flame conjured from the Wizard's hand. The flame formed into the shape of a prancing pony, and the warm glow beamed off the delighted face of a sick, smiling child.

"Will she live?" Drugar asked as the Witch Doctor limped over and dropped a bag of medicine at his feet.

"For a time," she smiled, revealing teeth as crooked as the mountain she lived on, "But one can say that for everyone."

"Hah." Drugar grabbed the bag of medicine and dropped a purse of gold in return. "Let us hope the time is warm, at least." He shot another look into the fire lit hovel, shined a grin, and ambled down the cold slope.

Time Web Gambit

The corridor reeked of infinity. High walls reached into the ether, coated by currents of power flowing heavenwards into the cosmic abyss. The walls ran along the un-spooling web of time that shifted and glitched with pulses of energy. The web spun down the unending hall, each white tendril a scattering of potential, vibrating from one instance of reality to the next and back again, only coalescing in fixed points with other tendrils when bundled together by the Time Keeper.

The shifting, partly bound universe had been tended to like a vine curling around a lattice, guided along its growth throughout the ages.

"Who bundles the timelines?" Freidnick asked. The Time Keeper ignored him as he guided him along the chaotic time web. Freidnick prodded him with the crossbow. "Don't forget, I'm not afraid to use this."

The Time Keeper sighed and turned to face his captor; his technicoloured cloak rippled with the motion and hid his face. "I am aware, however, I'm not aware of how you arrived here with your sanity intact."

"I already went insane when Kreit died . . . are we close?"

The Time Keeper hesitated, the silence filled with the thrumming power of the web as it shifted and crackled. "It's not far," he gestured for them to continue.

"Why bind sections of the time web?" Freidnick asked.

"Each tendril you see represents potential sequences of events. If it flickers upwards, an earthquake destroys a city. Downwards, the city planner built a city strong enough to survive. To the left, no earthquake at all . . . . Infinitesimally small variations of just one tendril's path could spell infinite events. Where I have bundled happenings, it was because the worst potential of a tendril was too severe to risk. I direct the sequence to something more survivable to negate the risk of utter catastrophe."

"But catastrophes happen, old man."

The Time Keeper laughed, "Aye, but life perseveres. Sometimes, in binding a tendril away from disaster, another tendril must be bound into a lesser disaster. It is my duty to choose the lesser evils. For instance," he stopped at a binding of red cord, "Here a volcano could blanket the world in darkness, but I bound it away from that. Now the volcano simply smoulders, but only if it binds another tendril in an unfortunate place. Now across the sea a rebellion slaughters many . . . it is difficult."

"But the volcano is not destined to erupt without intervention. There is infinite potential if it's left untended. You could take that risk and not condemn a nation to war."

"No, the volcano may not destroy the world if time was left to run its own course. But that is too high a risk to take."

After a time, they came to a bundled knot, the white crackling of time potentiality raged against the binding.

"What is this?" Freidnick asked.

"This is the point in time where Kreit was murdered."

"It's bound . . . you did this?"

"Yes," The Time Keeper nodded. "To prevent a great evil from rising, I bound the tendril in place with your friend's death."

Freidnick drew his knife.

"What are you doing?" The Time Keeper started.

"If I cut the cord, the separate tendrils split into infinite potential. The evil may not be, but Kreit may live."

"It's too great a risk!"

"Have faith in our ability to decide our own fate. We can sail the tendrils of time to bring about a different outcome. For him, it's a risk I'll take!" Freidnick slashed the cord.

The bundle snapped and the bound currents of time exploded into a shifting multitude of infinites. Now evil had a chance to reign, but his friend had a chance to live.

It was a gambit worth the risk.

The Gardener and the Tea Mage

The wind chimes sounded lazy dulcet tones in the gentle breeze. It spread a smile across the woman's crinkled face. She sighed, digging through pot plants to remove weeds from her little paradise in the small walled garden.

The chimes were quickly drowned out by a jackhammer, then a car horn. The tranquillity faded.

"I hate this place," she stood and groaned.

Her children meant well, packing her up and shipping her into the city. It was so they could keep an eye on her now that she was alone. But she was miserable.

The compost bin was too far away to bother. Shoving the weeds into her apron pocket, she tore off her gloves, tossed them on the table, and hobbled into her tiny home.

"Bugger, no tea."

She grabbed her walking stick, removed the apron from her neck and wrapped it around her waist, bracing herself for the streets. The city was built from red brick and wrought iron, lit warmly in the afternoon sun, which she enjoyed.

But no one else slowed down to enjoy it. Rushing pedestrians flowed around her like water around stone.

She stopped across from the supermarket, busy, too busy. She sighed, but noticed a hanging sign in the shape of a teacup swaying down the street.

Odd, she hadn't noticed that before.

Intrigued, she hobbled over. An entrance led down shallow steps into a basement. It brimmed with the scent of steaming brews, with comfy seats lit by lamps, and windows set into the wall tops in line with the footpath outside.

"Welcome," the tea maker beckoned her down the stairs. He was an elderly gentleman with a warm smile. "Have a seat."

She sat with a sigh as he hobbled over.

"A newcomer," he said, "Liking my humble shop?"

"It is a bit bare," she smiled. It had nothing but worn art lining the brickwork. "Could use some greenery."

"Sadly, I have none."

Smirking, she pulled the weeds from her apron. "A small start."

The tea maker took them reverently and placed them in a cup by the window. "They will be beautiful!"

She chuckled, "They're only weeds, and not usually what people display."

"Nonsense. They are hardy and beautiful for surviving in such a place, even if no one appreciates them." He gestured to the passing feet on the footpath through the basement windows. He wiggled his fingers over the cup which filled with soil. The weeds grew tall and blossomed with flowers.

She gasped, and he winked at her.

"I tell you what. You bring me a cutting every time you come here, and I'll give you a free cuppa."

"Sounds . . ." she hesitated, but not from fear of the magic she witnessed, ". . . Like a deal."

The place was quiet and cosy and the man seemed nice, lonely and, in search of a friend to accompany him in his little paradise.

She was happy to oblige.

As the days passed into weeks, the shop teemed with green irregularities. They would spend whole afternoons in friendly companionship as the world passed by outside.

SOLACE ON DESOLATE HILL

Gavrat leaned heavily on his gnarled stick. He gripped it firmly, grinding his hands, which displaced the last few minutes' buildup of dust from between his gloved fingers.

Then he adjusted the mask on his face. The goggles had fogged up again, but he was nowhere near shelter for the moment.

But they would clear soon enough, and his poor lungs couldn't take one breath of this pollution if he tried to remove it..

He pulled his hood down low and set off up the hill. The abrasive winds whipped his heavy cloak, which would pull the old fella off balance if not for his stick. For the millionth time, he thought the ironic thought, not in rage or sorrow like before, but in quiet lamentation.

He had always thought the dystopian future the lunatics raved about would be unbreathable and require masks. But from manmade smog, exhaust and constant grey due to the obstructing layers that pilfered the sky.

He was almost right.

This *was* manmade. This once lush, hilly area was a place of damp black earth and green brush. The brush swayed in the gentle winds as droplets from the recent rains were flung sporadically from their ferns.

Now—after years of horrendous fires and drought— it had turned to desert and petrified wood.

We knew this would happen. The roots withered, and the soil blew away in the wind. If the sky was not obscured by smoke, it was obscured by dust. Instead of a grey veil, the people of this land were smothered with red-orange sepia tones. It turned the skin gaunt and the soul lean.

But even as Gavrat lamented the loss of what he remembered as a child, he saw hope all around him. He passed the hydroponic sheds, connected by tunnels of precious soil and conduits for surviving bees, insects, and the like to travel between artificial paradises. All powered by looming wind turbines, dark in the hazing distance.

He found on his climb a dome encased *water feature*. Someone had taken the time to sieve out the finer particles of sand from the earth and created a cascading flow of dust. The sediment was air blasted through a separate chamber back up to the top to cascade down again in a mesmerising dance.

The ingenuity cracked a smile on the old fella's lips.

The sepia turned to deep red and then to stifling darkness as the sun set somewhere up above, and Gavrat found his look out.

His mother used to bring him here. They would look out over the city and the phalanx of lights would dazzle him senseless.

Now they were dimmed and marred by the smoke screen, enclosed by the scorched earth and encroaching grey skeleton forests. Yet he found some hope still, even as he massaged his old joints and beat the buildup of dust from his respirator.

The people still lived, thrived and pushed on, they still worked to counteract the waste their ancestors left them, even though it was through no fault of their own.

The lights may have been obscured, but they still shone.

THE MOUNTAIN SPIRIT

Wet winds whirled with cool mists and refreshing chill up upon the ridges, whistling pleasantly against the crags high above the green country. Soft blankets of fog clung lazily to the grey peaks and rolled over the slopes before catching in the gale and flitting across the sky. Moss clung to damp rock with the clean smell of wet earth along the trail and a single climber ascended through the majesty with aching lungs and a hobbled gait.

He tripped over a stray branch and cried out, slamming into the cold ground with a final grunt of despair.

"This is pointless!" He spat the bitter taste of soil from his mouth and noticed a flat section of rock to rest on. He crawled out from the trail and onto the level ridge that overlooked the vista. "What am I even doing up here?" He slumped down.

"What indeed?"

The climber flinched and scanned the area. The voice came from . . . everywhere? It whistled in the winds, and emerged from the rolling fogs, and reverberated from the deep roots of the mountain all at once.

"Who goes there?"

"You might say I go nowhere, in your understanding. I am the thing on which you tread, turn around friend, and see me."

The climber stood and turned slowly, trepidation slowing his movement more than his hobble ever could. He gazed up as horror seized his breath. The crags and crevices of the ridge formed a titanic face on the mountain, a mottled, gnarled thing which stared down at the climber with concern.

"Behold, the mountain!"

"It's, it's," the climber collapsed, scrambling away until he felt the edge of the ridge and remembered the eerily inviting heights, "It's not possible."

"Not possible?" The face did not move as it spoke, but the expression changed somehow, without being seen, to one of amusement. "Not possible that something so ancient and persistent throughout the ages should have a voice, a face? But in your mind, it is entirely possible that a tiny, short-lived creature, such as yourself, should come to understand the universe?"

"I guess that's fair," he suddenly felt very small, "Are you friendly?"

"I have not thrown you from my skin so far, have I?" The face changed without moving again, the expression morphing with impossibility.

"I guess that's also fair." The climber sighed and let his body sag.

"What troubles you, little creature? Why do you persist to my summit despite your injury?"

"What good am I if I cannot even manage a simple walk?"

The mountain laughed, the sound rolling up from its roots and all the way into the climber's bones. "Simple? Is that what you call it when a poor creature, alone, in pain, and in tears, braves the elements that cause it discomfort? Your journey may have been simple to start, but I know not why you persist in it."

"I said I would do it. I promised myself I would do it, that I *could* do it!"

"And failure would lessen you?"

"Yes!" The expression in the rock face morphed, without motion again, into bemusement. The climber looked away abashed, "No."

"Then why punish yourself, friend?"

"I was supposed to prove to myself that I could accomplish something. And now look at me."

"I *am* looking at you," the enormity of the being weighed down on the climber, "And I am looking past you, to the beautiful vista that your *failure* has allowed you to view. Go on, friend, look."

The climber sighed and gazed out over the country. He was struck by the green fields, punctuated by the terracotta roofs of the quaint towns that inhabited them, and the rivers that spread across the land. They glistened like sapphire veins in the golden sun that burned through the wispy fog, leaving him dazzled with awe.

"So you did not accomplish the arbitrary goal you set, but you still gained something beautiful. And not just the view, you have clear air, exercise, isolation, self reflection. These are also gifts. Maybe you can't conquer the physical mountain, but there are many more challenges that lay ahead. People will die, limbs will fracture, and hearts will break. Your home may flood, or be torn from you in the gale while your livelihood goes up in flames. These are all mountains to climb. In doing so, you will become stronger, in mind and body and spirit. No matter how high you ascend, you will be granted some reward for the effort. You just need to remember to look."

"So the mountains will come even if I wish not to climb them, even if I am not ready, like today?"

"That is my nature, my friend."

"Hardly seems fair."

The face morphed to mirth. "And that is life's nature, I'm afraid. But despite these trials, you will always be able to find some slither of joy."

"I don't understand."

"Understanding, too, is a mountain, and I look forward to when you ascend it so that we may speak again. Until then, stop punishing yourself, recognise your achievement and go get that ankle looked at." With that, the face vanished from the climber's perception.

He searched the ridge and scrutinised the crags in disbelief. The line that formed the eye was just a shadow, the nose was just a boulder and the lips just a crevice. No matter how he squinted or tilted his head, he could not make the shapes form a face again.

"I wonder if I'm mad." He shuffled from the ridge to start his descent, finding that the branch he tripped over was smooth and the perfect height to use as a cane to aid his injury. Smiling, he stooped to pick it up, gazing out over the vista once more. "You're right," he said. "Perhaps this is enough."

JUST ONE MORE

Fresh blood turned the dust in my mouth to mud. I gripped at the ground, but my ring finger would not bend. At least it was too numb for me to know why. My opponent—an eldritch tormentor—kicked me onto my back.

I was exposed to the scorching sun that bore through the roaring hum of billions of fighting rings.

The beast loomed over me, the silhouette of a nightmarish shape beneath the light, and I shielded myself with my all but broken hand. Beams of light pierced through splayed fingers and lashed at tender skin.

This was it.

It heaved and lifted its ungodly fists.

The bell rung out across the brawling tapestry, a low hum through the throng. The round was over.

With a derisive snort, the beast returned to its corner, and I crawled back to mine. By trembling hands, I hauled myself up and heaved over the side, gazing out across the people who survived their own bouts, and those who did not.

Some thrived, some were haggard, but many were as broken as me. But what set bile to my coarse throat, what set my heart burning with nigh spent fury, were the rings where some had finished their fights and enjoyed the spoil for their toil.

I had fought as hard as them. I had suffered as they had suffered, even more so than some.

Why?

How many rounds must I endure before I was free or slaughtered?

The foul adjudicators shuffled throughout the rings, dispensing decrees and the like. A creature looked me over and shrugged, moving on. The woman opposite me was deemed finished. She collapsed in relief and my furious bile burned hotter.

Why?

How many more rounds must I endure?

The bell rung out across the arenas.

The next round was beginning.

I contemplated not moving, leaning against the ropes as the fighter across from me enjoyed her respite ... Despite myself, I felt some relief on her behalf. Then my gaze drifted across those who fought alongside me in their own rings, and across those of the dead.

I knew the answer, as much as I hated it.

Why? *Because I must.*

I pushed off and stumbled into the centre of the ring against my eldritch tormentor. It snorted and readied to rush me.

I raised my fists . . .

How many more rounds must I endure?

Perhaps, just one more.

KNIGHT WALK

The battle was a catastrophic defeat. The rebels were scattered and now Laurein was running for her life . . . well . . . *running* was a strong word. In the chaos, only one of the King's soldiers had managed to pursue her. He was a knight, trained from a young age to kill. Laurein knew she was no match for such a fighter. But with him being in full plate armour—and given he was chasing her up a hill—all he could manage was to march, *menacingly*, after her.

Laurein had given up running about twenty minutes ago. Instead, she plodded along, staying just beyond the reach of his sword.

"You'll have to give up some time!" He barked, waving his sword as he huffed and puffed after her. "This path leads to a dead end!"

"I know this area as well as you! I'm pretty sure you'll have a heart attack before we get there," Laurein called over her shoulder, sipping water from her leather satchel. "The hill steepens soon. You might want to save your energy."

The knight soldiered on in silence, save for the wheezing, which grew louder.

"May I have some water?" He finally asked.

"No."

"Then I am defeated." The knight stopped mid stride and collapsed backwards, the clanging of his armour following him as he tumbled down the slope.

Laurein watched him go, and wiped the sweat from her brow. "Thank God for that. We were almost at the top."

THE ONE TRUE RAT

The deluge pelted against cold concrete on an almost empty train platform, blotting the last of the fading twilight. Harsh lights pierced the cascade, illuminating a patchwork of glistening dark furs, glinting eyes, and bristling whiskers.

Short-tail's matted fur clumped in a shaggy tangle as he stalked through the assembled swarm of rats. They parted for him as he pattered in sync with the rain, making his way towards Tooth-king and his snivelling rat minions.

"Tooth-king!" Short-tail bellowed.

A tongue of lightning licked the skies, reflecting in dappled brilliance off the puddles on the platform. A crack of thunder followed in its wake, quieting the snarl of Tooth-king's guard.

A giant, silver rat leered with one unscarred eye at Short-tail from the top of his bounty—a discarded hotdog in its bun—left to soak in the rain.

"Newcomer?" Tooth-king snarled, "What would the wanderer from the city have of his new king?"

"This food should belong to the swarm in equal measure. It is not your right to claim so much for you and your chummy rats!"

The swarm of rats chattered and squeaked amongst themselves. The king's minions looked from the masses to their leader.

"That is not the way of a true rat!" Tooth-king snarled as another lick of lightning tore the skies in two. "You do not know our ways!"

Short-tail sighed, he had hoped it would not come to this, "I am more rat than you are. I challenge you, Tooth-king, to single combat for the right to the hotdog!"

"Then you will die and add to my feast!" Tooth-king leaped from the hotdog, landing a savage swipe across Short-tail's face.

Short-tail screamed and responded, dicing the king's shoulder and neck with a flurry of short, sharp strikes.

Tooth-king snarled and faltered back under Short-tail's barrage, age and battle scars faltering to youth.

The brawl took them to the edge of the platform, and Short-tail spun, whipping the tip of his tail against Tooth-king's good eye. Tooth-king cried out in despair, rearing onto his hind legs as he recoiled, and Short-tail rammed him, toppling him over the edge.

"The King is dead!" Short-tail rounded on the other rats. "This food is for all!"

Without hesitation, the rats swarmed upon the hotdog, and the beleaguered Short-tail watched with a smile.

Sometime later, a human entered the platform, carrying a large box and an extendable rubbish picker. He stepped around the corpses of rats until he came to the only one left alive.

"Well Short-tail," he said, "You kept your end of the deal. You made the rats eat the poison . . . I don't get how you could betray your kind like that." He removed a large wedge of cheese as he spoke and tossed it to Short-tail, who caught it in two grubby hands.

"I am a true rat, dear rat catcher. I'll meet you in the next town."

A NOTE FROM THE AUTHOR

Thanks for reading Whacky, Whimsical & Dark!

Your review would make my day! An honest review on Amazon or Goodreads helps other readers find this story, and keeps me writing books for amazing readers like you.

Want more?

Read a collection of _horror_ short stories in **"Grim, Ghastly & Gripping"** available now!

Visit **SEANMTS.COM** to:

- Get a free eBook (and audio stories) when you join the community newsletter

- Read free short stories and articles

- Discover more books you might love

- Stay in contact on Instagram: @seanmtshanahan

- Email: sean@seanmts.com

If you enjoyed this collection, you will love my other books. You can find an up to date list on my site.

Thanks again.

Take care,

Sean

ABOUT THE AUTHOR

Sean M. T. Shanahan is a Science Fiction and Fantasy author from Sydney, Australia. He is known for writing emotionally gripping, high-stakes stories that blend dynamic characters with intriguing concepts and take you through darkness into the light.

He has a lifelong passion for storytelling, and since publishing his first book in 2021 has produced multiple books that span Fantasy, Steampunk, Sci-Fi, and children's fiction.

Drawing inspiration from history, science, mythology, and adventure, he weaves immersive tales that will pull you in from the start and leave you wanting more.

Besides reading and writing, Sean enjoys nature, gaming, parkour, endurance sports, and making terrible jokes.

www.ingramcontent.com/pod-product-compliance
Lightning Source LLC
Chambersburg PA
CBHW040228170726
48295CB00014B/849